Readers love the Club Whisper series by XENIA MELZER

A Dom and His Writer

"The writing is vivid with all the best emotions and feels. This was a heartwarming and entertaining read with a bit of angst and hot chemistry. Highly recommended."

—Love Bytes

"It's been a long time since I've stayed up until the early hours of the morning reading a book, but this one had me hooked."

—Open Skye Book Reviews

"This author had me intrigued from the get-go, and I had a hard time putting it down. I fell in love with the characters, the storyline and it had the perfect amount of hot sex."

—OptimuMM

A Dom and His Artist

"A really enjoyable read that brought home the fact that BDSM is not about a set of rules that cannot be broken, but about finding the right set of rules…."

—Two Chicks Obsessed

"Ms. Melzer does an amazing job of character creation …"

—The Romance Reviews

By Xenia Melzer

Love Wins

CLUB WHISPER
A Dom and His Writer
A Dom and His Artist
A Dom and His Warrior

Published by Dreamspinner Press
www.dreamspinnerpress.com

A DOM AND HIS WARRIOR

XENIA MELZER

Published by

DREAMSPINNER PRESS

5032 Capital Circle SW, Suite 2, PMB# 279, Tallahassee, FL 32305-7886 USA
www.dreamspinnerpress.com

A Dom and His Warrior
© 2018 Xenia Melzer.

Cover Art
© 2018 Aaron Anderson.
aaronbydesign55@gmail.com
Cover content is for illustrative purposes only and any person depicted on the cover is a model.

Trade Paperback ISBN: 978-1-64080-677-1
Digital ISBN: 978-1-64080-678-8
Library of Congress Control Number: 2018935335
Trade Paperback published September 2018
v. 1.0

Printed in the United States of America

This paper meets the requirements of
ANSI/NISO Z39.48-1992 (Permanence of Paper).

To all the chocolate lovers out there.

Acknowledgments

WRITING A book is pretty easy, at least according to my favorite author, Terry Pratchett. All you need is a beginning, a middle, and an end…

Well, yes, those are good starting points. You also need an understanding spouse and children who don't get sick too often, good friends to cheer you on when you're having one of those days where you contemplate just deleting it all, and a sister who will read your manuscript and very kindly point out all the logical mistakes you made. You also need good editors, like Anne, Kelly, Anastasia, and Liv, who put up with your recurring grammar mistakes (strangely enough, punctuation is NOT optional), find all the mistakes your sister has missed, and still feel kind enough to leave a few encouraging comments in the manuscript so you don't get depressed.

Furthermore, you need chocolate. Lots of it. The dark kind. And peppermint tea with honey. And somebody to massage your feet. If you have all those things, you can write a book just like that. Ha, ha.

CHAPTER 1

JONATHAN'S GAZE wandered lovingly over Leeland's naked body. They were at Whisper, in a private suite, for an intense session. Over the past three weeks, they hadn't had much time for each other, and tonight was all about reconnecting. It was also about stress relief. Leeland's end-of-semester exams were over. His boy had done well; no, more than well, straight As. One more year of hard work and Leeland would finish college. Jonathan drew a deep breath, focusing on Leeland's perfect body in the sling. A black, silken blindfold kept his boy from seeing what he was doing. Leeland's breathing was even, though. He trusted Jonathan completely.

It always humbled Jonathan, that trust. Especially when he thought how easily Leeland could toss him on his ass thanks to his martial arts training. The heady feeling of exerting power over somebody so strong had Jonathan's cock swelling in his leather trousers. Leeland's contradictions never failed to turn him on. That beautiful, slender body, the androgynous beauty, the long silken hair, the huge almond-shaped eyes, the pert little nose, and the thin yet sensual lips all appealed to Jonathan's protective instincts, his need to conquer and own, the urge to dominate.

The fierce intelligence, sassy mouth, and self-confidence backed up by a solid training in self-defense called out to Jonathan's inner predator, which had been seeking an equal for so long. Yes, Leeland was everything Jonathan could wish for, everything he ever wanted. What he had planned for tonight was one way of showing Leeland how much Jonathan appreciated and loved him. Just thinking of the pleasures to come had Jonathan's cock dripping precum.

He circled the swing, making sure everything was secure, Leeland's wrists and ankles bound but not in a way that would hurt him. Even though they both enjoyed the occasional spanking, they were more into sensual play. Jonathan trailed his fingertips over Leeland's rib cage, reveling in the smoothness of the skin and the slight quiver the touch sent through Leeland's body. His boy moaned low, full of anticipation. Jonathan smiled.

"This is going to be so good, honey." He paused. "Your safeword?"

Leeland smiled. Jonathan knew he appreciated being asked every time they did a scene. It showed how much Jonathan cared, how seriously he took their interactions.

"Dust bunny for stop, dandelion for slow down, pasture for go."

"Very good. Let the games begin."

He knew how corny that sounded, and Leeland's giggle only confirmed it. With a determined expression, Jonathan went to the little table where he had laid out the things he needed for this session.

First he took the ostrich feather. There was nothing like a light warm-up before he went for the heavier ammunition, so to speak. He let the feather trail over Leeland's stomach, eliciting a groan from his boy. Jonathan smiled when he saw goose bumps rising on the lightly tanned skin. Mapping out Leeland's body with the feather, he went from his stomach to his right side, sliding the filaments along the rib cage, into the armpit, up the underside of Leeland's arm, then down again to repeat the same action on the other side. By the fourth time the feather started its journey, Leeland was squirming in his confines, making the sling swing. Jonathan put a hand on his boy's belly, stopping all movement.

"Shh, boy. We've only begun."

Leeland whimpered. "I know. Don't stop."

Jonathan bent forward and kissed the trembling lips, swallowed another needy moan. Then he went back to work, changing the path of the feather downward, over Leeland's slim waist, his slightly protruding hip bones, the long, shapely legs, up on the inside of his thighs, teasing his balls and cock, which twitched every time the feather ghosted over the hot, sensitive flesh. Leeland tried to arch his back, a futile exercise in the sling. The knowledge that he was doing this to his boy, that it was him who had Leeland moaning and whimpering and begging by using nothing more than a feather, went straight to Jonathan's groin, making his balls draw up and his own shaft try to punch a hole in his leathers. Leeland was utterly gorgeous when he gave in like that.

Jonathan let the feather trail over the swollen balls once more before he put it away and retrieved the next item on the table. Because he couldn't see, his boy was visibly straining his ears to guess what was coming next. Jonathan grinned and lifted the small porcelain bowl with the warm sandalwood-scented oil high in the air before he tipped it. The oil poured out in a small, controlled trickle, met Leeland's sensitized flesh with barely a sound, and started running down his torso, drawing happy moans from Leeland. Once the bowl was empty, Jonathan placed it back on the table before he started massaging the oil into Leeland's body, thoroughly enjoying the act. He was an extremely sensual man who loved giving that kind of pleasure. Jonathan had to admit, though, that he had never before met a sub who reveled in it like Leeland did. With him everything got ramped up almost indefinitely. Now, too, he tried to arch into Jonathan's touch, begging, whimpering, moaning, baring himself to anything Jonathan wanted to give him. It was like a drug—for both of them.

Jonathan alternated firm strokes with featherlight touches of his fingertips, never stopping until Leeland's skin felt heated under his fingers. He grinned a tiny bit evilly. The next part would have Leeland fighting for control. He bent down and whispered close to his boy's ear.

"Remember, honey, no coming unless I say so."

Leeland groaned, the words alone making his cock twitch. Jonathan watched his boy squirm for a bit; then he went to the table again. Carefully, drawing out the moment for both his and his fidgeting boy's sake, he selected one of the ice cubes sitting in another bowl. The sudden coldness felt good on his fingers, and he could only imagine what Leeland would experience.

He took the cube, went back to Leeland, and hovered above his nipples, waiting for the drops of water to fall. When the first one hit the heated skin of Leeland's nicely pebbled nipple, the boy hissed in a combination of pleasure and surprise.

"Damn."

Jonathan cleared his throat. Another drop fell, closely followed by a third and fourth.

"Sorry, Master. Aah!"

Leeland whimpered, and Jonathan put the entire cube on his left nipple. When Jonathan started drawing circles around both nipples, leaving a wet trail behind, eventually venturing upward toward Leeland's neck and ears, then downward again, passing the valley of his navel and heading for his groin, he got a steady stream of moans and whimpers that turned into incoherent begging once he reached Leeland's swollen nuts. The ice cube was almost gone. Jonathan dipped it into his navel, leaving it to melt completely, before he got another one from the bowl, going straight back to Leeland's sex. He teased the hard shaft, slipped it over the weeping slit, dragged it down over the balls, rubbing the sensitive flesh between balls and hole before he began massaging Leeland's pucker.

Carefully, so as not to lose his grip on the cube, Jonathan pushed it against the tight ring of muscle, teasing, challenging, and Leeland sang for him, his breath coming in short gasps. The muscles in his thighs trembled, and his hole started to open for the cube. Jonathan slid the ice inside, rubbing it around, pushing it deeper until it was completely melted. He got another cube and repeated the action. Leeland's inner passage was now cold to the touch, and he bucked against the two fingers Jonathan had inside him.

"Please! Jonathan, please!"

It wasn't the urgency in Leeland's voice that convinced Jonathan it was time to fuck him. It was Leeland calling him by his name. When Leeland was close to flying, he always stopped addressing Jonathan as Master and went for his name instead. Other Doms might have taken offense, but Jonathan loved it. He loved that he could wreck Leeland so completely that he forgot all protocol.

Quickly Jonathan opened his leathers, poured some oil on his cock, and slicked himself up. With a sigh he stepped between Leeland's spread legs in the swing.

"I'm going to give it to you now, honey."

He got a sob for an answer. Jonathan placed one hand on Leeland's stomach; with the other, he lined himself up. Slowly, carefully, he pressed the head of his cock into Leeland's hole and hissed when the cold hit him. So good. This was so good. Leeland moaned.

"More. Jonathan, I need more! Fuck me!"

That, too, was something most Doms didn't tolerate, a sub who told them what to do. But who was he to refuse his gorgeous angel after he had been so good? Jonathan pressed deeper, until he was fully seated inside Leeland's ass. For a moment he stilled, enjoyed the sensation of Leeland's still cool passage gripping him firmly, slowly heating up again. When Leeland made an impatient sound, he started fucking him with long, sure movements, trying to draw it out as long as possible.

It was difficult, though. There was just so much sensation, combined with the giddy knowledge that they weren't separated by a barrier. Only that afternoon they had gotten their test results, and Jonathan still couldn't believe he was doing this, riding his boy bareback. His. They were exclusive. Just the two of them.

Leeland seemed to be equally aroused, because he panted some incoherent words.

"We. Bare. Harder. So good. More."

Jonathan grabbed Leeland's hips with both his hands and started fucking him in earnest. They wouldn't last long, so why torture himself? He wasn't the sub in this relationship. When Jonathan felt the warning tingling in his back, he growled low.

"Come, Leeland! Now!"

Leeland made a choking sound, and with Jonathan's next brutal inward stroke, they came together, Leeland spraying his seed on his belly, the spurts going as far as his chin, Jonathan releasing deep inside his lover's body and slumping down on him in a heap of bliss.

As far as Jonathan was concerned, this was heaven.

CHAPTER 2

AFTER A few moments of sated silence, Leeland groaned and wiggled under Jonathan's weight. Jonathan propped himself up, which wasn't as easy with the sling as it would have been on a bed. He actually had to work his back muscles here. He felt his softening cock slipping out of Leeland's body.

"Hmm, honey, wanna plug you."

"Perv."

"Admit it, you love me for it. Besides, this is the first time we went bareback. I want to trap my cum inside you."

Thanks to the blindfold, Jonathan wasn't able to see the eye roll Leeland was surely giving him right now, and therefore didn't have to punish his sweet sub.

"How caveman can you get? I'm not a woman. There won't be any babies, you know that, don't you?"

Jonathan grinned and slapped Leeland's flank hard enough to remind him of their roles.

"Brat. Now clench that sweet hole of yours while I go looking for a nice fat plug."

He slipped completely from Leeland's hole and admired the view for a moment. The pucker was a beautiful pink, glistening with oil and cum and twitching helplessly. Jonathan felt his own shaft taking a renewed interest. *Plug*, he reminded himself. *Plug and then aftercare.* He rummaged in one of the drawers in the playroom, grateful that Whisper provided all kinds of sex toys. With a triumphant huff, he selected a moderate-sized silicone plug in neon yellow, sauntered back to the sling where Leeland was still waiting, squeezing his hole to keep Jonathan's spunk from flowing out, and pushed it into his sub. Leeland moaned, his cock, too, perking up again.

Jonathan removed the blindfold and pressed a quick kiss on Leeland's nose.

"Cuddle." Leeland was obviously still blissed out; his eyes had that glazed-over look that told Jonathan he would fall asleep soon. He hurried to get Leeland out of the sling and then carried him over to the king-size bed every private playroom at Whisper had. Jonathan arranged the pillows so he could lean comfortably against the headboard. With a contented sigh, he pulled Leeland between his legs. Leeland's head came to rest on his broad chest, the faint smell of his lemon shampoo mixing with the sandalwood from the oil and the more prominent scents of sex and sweat. When Jonathan reached for the wet wipes on the bedside table—another item every suite had—the sagging of Leeland's body told him that his boy was already asleep. Jonathan chuckled, wiped the drying cum from Leeland's stomach, tossed the soiled tissue in the general direction of the garbage bin, missed, and didn't care about it.

Meeting Leeland was the best thing that had ever happened to him. Jonathan had felt drawn to him from the moment he first saw Leeland's elegant, sleek body behind the bar of Whisper. They had a few scenes together, but at that time Jonathan had thought Leeland was like all the other submissives—submissive. And, yes, he knew how contradictory that idea was. At Richard's and Dean's housewarming party, he had approached Leeland from behind, and Leeland had tossed him on his ass without apparent effort. That had been enough reason for Jonathan to ask the boy on a date. From then on their relationship had steadily progressed to the point where they now went bareback. He was one lucky bastard, and he knew it.

Between his legs, Leeland stirred, yawned, and tried to snuggle even closer. Jonathan smiled softly, wrapping his arms around Leeland's torso.

"What an amazing scene, Master. So good."

Jonathan chuckled. He always enjoyed Leeland's evaluation of their scenes. Some Doms didn't like that, even felt insulted when their subs told them what they enjoyed or hated about a scene. Jonathan was grateful for the input. That way he was able to constantly improve and create even better experiences for both of them. It suited his competitive streak.

"So you liked it?"

"Hmm. A lot. I mean, a good spanking does have its merits, but this… this was something else. Hot and cold and hot…." He trailed off, stroking Jonathan's fingers in an absentminded way. "Sex without a condom is great too. I felt so connected."

Jonathan's heart did that crazy little dance he had learned to associate with Leeland, and he spoke without thinking.

"Move in with me."

In his arms Leeland went very still. Jonathan bit his lip, inwardly cursing himself. Why, oh why did he have to blurt that out? It was something he had been mulling over for a month now, waiting for the right moment to propose. He hadn't meant to spring it on Leeland like this. After a scene was never a good time to discuss important matters. Too many hormones on the rampage.

"Honey?"

Leeland's lack of a response worried Jonathan. When he had pictured them living together, he had never once thought Leeland might be opposed to the idea. Reluctant, perhaps, but not opposed. Jonathan felt dread creeping up his spine.

Leeland started stroking his hand.

"Peyton's going to kill me. He's just finished decorating everything."

"*That's* your biggest concern?" Jonathan couldn't believe it. "I mean, you could be mad at me for springing this on you so suddenly, or overwhelmed because you never thought of it until now, or, I don't know, generally pissed because I blurted this out during aftercare. Yet you worry about Peyton's reaction?"

Leeland tilted his head sideways, grinning at Jonathan like a madman. When Jonathan saw the amused twinkle in Leeland's eyes, he knew he had walked right into that one.

Leeland chuckled, obviously seeing the understanding dawn on Jonathan's features.

"I'm not completely kidding. Yes, your proposal comes as a bit of a surprise, and, yes, you could have chosen the moment a bit more—carefully. But I've been thinking about moving in together as well. I spend a lot of time at your place already, and it's close enough to Dade and Whisper that commuting isn't a problem. Unfortunately, Peyton *is* going to kill me when I move out now. He put a lot of effort into making the apartment perfect, and he somehow even managed to talk Richard into paying for it."

Leeland furrowed his brows. "I still don't know how he did it, though. I mean, Richard has already given me the apartment, which is beyond generous. I didn't even know it was him paying the bill until Peyton slipped. Till then, I had bought his story that he was doing this for free in exchange for taking pictures from the apartment for his website."

Jonathan bit his lip. He remembered the day Leeland had found out about Richard paying the bill. His sweet boy had called the owner of Whisper immediately, telling him he didn't have to go so far and trying to talk him into at least splitting the bill. Richard had flat-out refused. After about twenty minutes of ranting on Leeland's side, Richard put an end to the call, using his Dom voice. Leeland had relented, though Jonathan knew he wasn't happy. Two days later, Jonathan had met Richard and asked him about the whole incident. As it turned out, it was Dean who paid Peyton to do the interiors for Leeland's apartment. Dean was beyond grateful for Leeland's help and support during his falling-out with Richard and had wanted to show his appreciation without endangering their friendship over something as mundane as money. After Peyton's slipup and subsequent blaming of Richard, Richard had agreed to be Dean's beard. Normally Jonathan didn't approve of this kind of scheming, but it was for his beloved boy, and nobody knew better than him how stubborn Leeland could be. He deserved everything. Dean had found a way to give him at least a good portion of everything, and Jonathan wasn't going to argue with that.

"It's fine, honey. You can always tell Peyton it's my fault."

Leeland wiggled around until he was on his knees, facing Jonathan, an impish smile brightening his face.

"You do know he's going to make you pay for it in some truly horrendous way, don't you?"

Jonathan huffed.

"I'm not afraid of Peyton."

"Because you don't know him that well—yet."

Leeland's voice sounded ominous enough to have Jonathan a tiny bit worried. Peyton had been to his own apartment once when

Jonathan had been thinking about renovating. Peyton's proposal of what could and should be done with the rooms had been enough to scare Jonathan off changing anything.

Sensing his distress, Leeland pressed a kiss on Jonathan's mouth. "Don't worry. He's probably just going to have a hissy fit. Don't talk back, and remember to say 'Yes, Peyton' at the appropriate moments, and you're fine."

Jonathan huffed. "I'm a Dom. I can deal with a thin streak of nothing like Peyton."

Leeland laughed out loud. "Of course you can, *Master*." He spread his legs, wincing a bit when the plug inside him seemed to graze his sweet spot, and settled on Jonathan's thighs. "You're my Master. My Dom. I love you."

Jonathan kissed his boy deeply.

"And I love you. Does that mean yes?"

"Yes! Gladly."

Jonathan pressed Leeland closer. With the fingers of his right hand, he nudged the base of the plug, sending another shiver through Leeland's body.

"Once you have your license, you can have one of the Harleys to drive to Dade and Whisper."

Leeland made a surprised sound. "Really?"

"Yes, boy. Anything to make your life with me comfortable." Jonathan could understand Leeland's surprise. His Harleys were his most prized possessions. But Jonathan had realized more than half a year ago that Leeland was even more precious to him. And he would soon have his license.

"My life with you is perfect. You just keep making it better and better."

"Keep the compliments up and my head is going to explode."

Leeland chuckled. "Don't worry. If you get too conceited, I can always challenge you to a round in the gym. That should reduce you to a reasonable size."

"Such a sweet-talker."

Jonathan knew he stood no chance against Leeland in a fight unless he managed to pin him down with his weight. Usually Leeland was too quick on his feet for that to happen. Having such a strong, self-reliant man submit to him, love him, put up with him, was more than Jonathan deserved, and he had every intention of showing Leeland for the rest of their lives how much he appreciated and loved him.

They started kissing, and soon the plug was replaced by something a lot more enjoyable for them both.

CHAPTER 3

"HI, LEELAND, Emilio! It's so good to see you!"

Leeland couldn't help but smile at Collin's eager greeting. The scatterbrained artist was a real doll.

"Hi, Collin. Thank you for having us!"

Collin hugged first Leeland, then Emilio. "Don't mention it. I'm so excited. The others are already here, and Martin is over at Richard's place, and I ordered food from Mamma's all on my own, and Dean was right, it really is easy, and we're going to have pasta and salad and tons of dessert, because dessert is just the best, and Martin has set up the TV for me so I only have to press two buttons."

Leeland grinned. For a typical Collin sentence, this one was fairly short. "I'm looking forward to it."

They followed the happily bouncing Collin into the huge villa where he and his Dom, Martin Carmichael, co-owner of Club Whisper, lived. Leeland made sure Emilio stayed close to his side. The pretty sub with the dark eyes and sinful lips seemed hesitant, which Leeland could relate to. Martin's house was huge, the immense wealth of its owner displayed in every little detail, from the polished antique-brass knobs on the doors to the gleaming hardwood floors and sparsely displayed trinkets that screamed money. And that was only the hall. The only thing that dimmed the intimidating feeling a bit were the sketchbooks, brushes, crayons, and pencils scattered around. Leeland knew Martin wanted Collin to keep his art in the conservatory that was his atelier, but it was an impossible demand. Collin worked wherever the muse struck him, and if it happened to be the hall, then he started sketching there, usually forgetting about tidying up afterward. They all had learned to walk carefully in Collin's home. Slipping on a pencil was *not* funny. On their way to where the others were, they passed a wall that had been blank the last time Leeland had visited. Now it sported a huge sketch of a naked man with half-spread wings, a collar around his neck, and a chain in his hands. The end of the chain was drawn in a way that it turned into a flock of butterflies flying along the wall. There wasn't any color yet, but the drawing was already mesmerizing.

"This is beautiful, Collin."

Collin stopped and looked at the wall with his head tilted to the right.

"I know. We were just back from Whisper a few days ago, and when Martin opened the door, I saw some moths dancing in the light above the entrance, and it struck me how much wings are connected to subs, and how important it is to fly, and how the chains really help us, how it all transcends, and I couldn't stop drawing, and I already know what colors I need, and I'm so glad Martin said it was okay to use the wall, because it just has to be here, and I can't imagine it being on canvas for some reason, though I need to get some real chains to work into it."

Leeland smiled. It was cute how excited Collin became whenever he talked about his work. It was also refreshing to spend time with somebody who had such a unique view of the world.

Now Collin led them into the living room, where Dean, Richard's husband, Peyton, Dean's friend and interior design genius, and Curtis, gallery owner and Collin's agent, were lounging on the two gigantic cream-colored sofas dominating the room.

"Look who's here!"

Peyton jumped up from where he was seated to hug first Leeland, then Emilio. Dean and Curtis followed his example. From the corner of his eye, Leeland watched as Dean embraced Emilio. The young man stiffened for a moment before he relaxed. When Dean's parents had tried to take his niece—now daughter—Emily away from him almost a year ago, they had hired a PI to find incriminating proof that Dean and Richard weren't able to take care of a baby. Because the security at Whisper was too tight for an outsider to just walk in, the PI threatened Emilio and forced him to take pictures of Dean and Richard in their leathers at Whisper. Emilio had been smart enough not to photograph anything explicitly sexual, figuring the pictures would then be worthless, which was the reason Richard and Martin hadn't fired him from his job at Whisper. He had received his punishment but was still a bit wary around Dean, as if he couldn't believe the writer had truly forgiven him. Leeland smiled. Dean was a generous man who had welcomed Emilio with open arms into their little gang of subs.

The doorbell rang, causing Collin to race outside again.

"The food!"

Only a few moments later, two men carried huge warming boxes with the logo of Mamma's on the side into the living room. The enticing smell made Leeland's mouth water. Curtis inhaled deeply, then furrowed his brows.

"Shouldn't we take this into the kitchen?"

Collin looked confused. "Why?"

"Because this is the living room, not the dining room?" Curtis gave the impression that he was trying to hold back a laugh.

Still, Collin didn't seem to understand. "We don't eat here?"

Dean slung an arm around Collin's waist. "It's your house, sweetie. We eat wherever you want. Mr. Gentleman over there just doesn't know you can eat in the living room. It's an alien concept to him."

Dean threw Curtis a mischievous smile, one the older man answered very maturely by sticking out his tongue.

Collin's eyes had become huge. "You don't eat in the living room?"

Curtis grinned. "As Dean said, this is your house. We eat where you want. I was merely—surprised by your choice of location."

Collin sighed in relief.

"I think it's nice to eat here. The couch is very comfortable. Peyton chose it. And today we don't have to worry about Dog stealing everything from our plates because Martin has taken him over to Richard's on a play date with Donar and Thor and Wilma and Fred, although he might be a bit disappointed because Dean said Emily is already asleep and Dog loves to play with her as well."

Leeland shared a look with Dean. It had been a surprise to everybody except Collin how well the sharp dog got along with the two dogs of Dean's father-in-law and the two cats Richard had gotten for Emily.

"Collin, sugar, we still need silverware and plates. I don't mind roughing it here, but I absolutely won't eat from the same crate as all of you. For that, there's not nearly enough alcohol involved." Peyton flashed his most charming smile. "And if any of you get a stain on the couch or the carpet, I'm going to string up your balls, and not in a good way."

When they all stared at him, he shrugged. "Hey, it was a nightmare getting those couches."

After that warning, Leeland helped Curtis and Collin to carry the cutlery into the living room. Peyton had already opened the different boxes, and the heavenly smell of pasta permeated the air.

Leeland licked his lips. "What have you gotten?"

Collin blushed. "I didn't know what everyone wanted, so I asked them to send over a selection of their pasta dishes, some salad, and lots of dessert."

"You mean lots of tiramisu." Leeland grinned when Collin looked at Dean for help.

"I think tiramisu is the perfect choice." Dean patted Collin's hand reassuringly. "If you don't want it, all the better. More for us."

"Hey, don't even dream about hogging all that creamy goodness! We want our share, am I right, Emilio?" Peyton nudged the youngest man in their midst with his elbow.

Emilio looked like a deer caught in the headlights. Leeland wasn't sure if Emilio was a shy person or if his years spent on the streets had made him that way. Now he was squirming under the combined attention of all the men.

"I… I probably shouldn't eat anything. Master Garrett has me on a strict diet."

Leeland furrowed his brows. In the back of his mind, an alarm started shrilling. Emilio had started doing scenes with Master Garrett about four months ago. Two months later, the master had asked him out on their first date. Until now Leeland had the impression that everything was going well between the two. Emilio seemed to thrive on the attention and care he received from Master Garrett.

"Why would he have you on a diet?" Curtis beat Leeland to the question.

Emilio blushed a deep red. "He wants to build up my stamina. For our scenes. He… Master Garrett can be very intense. He wants me to be able to get through the rougher scenes without passing out at the end. I'm going to his studio five times a week."

So that made sense and wasn't the bad scenario Leeland had anticipated. Still, it felt somehow off. As if Emilio wasn't entirely happy. Leeland could also see where Master Garrett was coming from. The man owned a string of high-class gyms all over the States. He was his own best advertisement, a perfectly built stud with not an ounce of fat marring his beautifully sculpted muscles. Emilio was— normal. He had the build of a young man who spent his time working and studying. Gym rat material he was not. Looking closer at him, Leeland detected some changes in Emilio's physique. His upper arms in the plain green polo shirt he wore seemed more defined, his chest a bit broader than it used to be. Yes, he was definitely training.

"Did he say anything about food restrictions for tonight? I mean, he must have known there would be food here." Dean sounded apprehensive.

Emilio shook his head. "He didn't say anything. But last time I failed to keep to the diet, he made me wear a cock cage throughout the weekend, fucking me whenever he pleased. Monday morning he took it off, sent me home, and forbade me to come for the entire week."

A collective wince came from Dean and Curtis. Leeland shuddered. Cock cages were mean. And Master Garrett was one of the strictest Doms at Whisper, even stricter than Richard and Martin, who were saps at heart and so firmly wrapped around Dean's and Collin's respective pinkies that it wasn't funny anymore. Jonathan had a bit more bite, but he, too, could easily be swayed with a pout or a pleading look. It was interesting how love could change a person.

"The question is, do you want to be punished?"

Peyton's voice tore Leeland from his musings. As always, the lively blond struck at the heart of the matter. Earning a punishment could be a fun thing, depending on the kind of punishment a Dom dished out. Even cock cages had their merits, though Leeland wasn't too keen on them.

Emilio seemed torn. "I don't know. He's so strict."

"I guess not telling him is out of the question?"

Peyton sounded matter-of-fact. Curtis shook his head.

"A sub doesn't lie to his master. At least, not in a functioning relationship. Absolute honesty is very important in BDSM."

"And you guys wonder why I don't want to give the pain ride a try." Peyton threw his hands in the air. "Make your choice, Emilio. Are you going to be naughty?"

The way Peyton said it had them all cracking a smile. Even Emilio, who still looked torn.

"Maybe just a bit. If it's only a small portion…."

"Okay, that's settled. I'm starving!"

With that Peyton grabbed a plate and started loading it with the different pasta variations. They all followed suit, Emilio included, who put about four strands of spaghetti *aglio e olio* on his plate before he settled down next to Leeland. For some time, happy silence ruled.

When their worst hunger was sated, or, at least Peyton's worst hunger, he looked around with an adventurous gleam in his eyes they all had come to dread.

"Any juicy news for us to chew on?"

Leeland tensed, hoping one of the others would come up with something outrageous that would keep them occupied the entire evening. He had no such luck. One after another, the men shook their heads. Collin and Martin were still discussing the perfect date for their wedding, and before that date was set, Martin had forbidden them to talk about the wedding itself because it worried Collin when he was confronted with so many choices. Leeland was almost sure Martin would hire a wedding planner at some point, just to keep his boy from stressing out. Even Dean didn't seem to have any news on the surrogate front, a topic that always kept them well-entertained. About five months ago, Richard and Dean had found a surrogate who was now trying to get pregnant. The first round had failed, and Dean was still disappointed. Hopefully the next try would be successful.

Leeland took a deep breath. He would have to tell them eventually, and with the others present, Peyton would perhaps not lose it completely.

"Uhm, I kind of… have news."

Leeland felt all eyes on him. A cold tingle ran up his spine. This was going to be a massacre.

"Jonathan asked me to move in with him and I—agreed."

The room erupted in chaos.

"Leeland, how wonderful! Congratulations!" That was Dean.

"Ohh, moving can be fun, you find so much stuff you never knew you had, it's like an adventure!" Collin added.

"Congratulations, Leeland. You and Jonathan are such a good couple. I'm sure this will be great." Curtis, kind and supportive as always, with a trace of sadness and longing in his eyes.

"That's great, Leeland." Emilio didn't say more. He was probably still agonizing over the three noodles he had consumed.

"What?" The shrill sound of Peyton's voice rose easily over the others. "I just spent *weeks* making the apartment perfect, and now you want to move out? And into that pigsty of all places? Have you *any* idea how long it took me to find the perfect color paint for the kitchen? Or to hunt down that dresser you said you liked so much? It was a nightmare, I can tell you. I had to drive down to this small backwater town whose name I can't even remember and haggle with an old witch who didn't want to let go of it because of 'sentimental value,' and I had to eat about a ton of her stone-hard cookies and talk until my tongue fell out before she finally agreed to sell it. And don't let me get started on the wooden tiles in your bedroom, or I'll have to kill you!"

Peyton's voice rose with every word until it reached a level close to what Leeland imagined a banshee's scream would sound like if the creatures existed. Leeland winced. This was bad.

"I'm sorry. Really. I know how hard you worked, and I appreciate it. A lot. It's just, this is the first time I'm moving in with somebody."

"Yeah, cut him some slack, Peyton. This is great news." Dean tried to mollify Peyton, for which Leeland was grateful.

Peyton looked hesitant for a moment, clearly weighing the benefit of keeping on with his tantrum against toning it down. A dangerous gleam entered his eyes. All of a sudden, Leeland felt like a mouse cornered by an athletic cat. No amount of self-defense training could have ever prepared him for Peyton when he was in one of his moods.

"Well, I may forgive you. Since my efforts on your apartment have clearly gone to waste, I could be persuaded not to be mad at you anymore when you give me free rein over Jonathan's apartment."

Leeland gulped. *Jonathan said he would do anything*, he reminded himself. How bad could it be? *You better kiss the Harley goodbye.* For a moment, Leeland wavered, but then he gave in. What choice did he have? He really wanted to live with his master.

"Fine. I'll tell Jonathan."

A satisfied smirk told Leeland how much he had just been played. He couldn't hold a grudge, though. Despite his capriciousness, Peyton was a good friend—and Jonathan's apartment could do with a little makeover. Well, not so little when Peyton was in charge, but it would increase the resale value dramatically. And if he kept on finding good reasons, he might end up believing one of them.

"Now that we've gotten this out of the way… Collin, what film have you chosen?"

Peyton seemed perfectly composed, probably because he had just gotten his way without much effort on his part. Leeland couldn't help but feel a tiny bit gleeful when Peyton saw the happy smile forming on Collin's lips, and his own face fell.

"No! Not *The Nightmare Before Christmas* AGAIN!"

Collin pouted. "Hey, that film is great. Don't worry, though. We're going to watch *Corpse Bride.*"

Now it was Curtis's and Dean's turn to groan.

"I always cry at the end of that film. Over somebody who's already dead!" Curtis almost whined.

"I've got tissues," suggested Collin helpfully.

Before Curtis could answer, Peyton chimed in. "You're one to talk. You made us watch *Eyes Wide Shut* last time we were at your place!"

"That film's a classic!" protested Curtis.

"Doesn't make it good. Next time we meet at my apartment."

Curtis huffed. "No way. I'm not going to sit through another Vin Diesel marathon."

Peyton rolled his eyes. "Vin is a stud."

"That may be the case, but his films are rubbish." Curtis's heated argument was backed up by a furiously nodding Dean.

Peyton held his hands up in protest. "Hey, just because there's not that much dialogue—"

"Try none," muttered Dean under his breath, which got him a glare from Peyton.

"—doesn't mean there's not a deeper meaning…."

"Oh please, what deeper meaning can there be in *The Fast and the Furious*?" Curtis sounded exasperated.

"Always wear a seat belt?" Emilio's voice was soft, shy, as if he wasn't sure how his statement would be taken.

For a moment there was stunned silence. Then the men started to laugh, Peyton included.

"Okay, I give you that." Peyton had tears in his eyes.

Emilio smiled shyly, clearly happy that his joke had been so well-received. Dean clapped him on the shoulder.

"How about we have a Colin Firth marathon next week? I think we can all agree on him being a stud and his films being suitably intellectual—well, most of them, anyway."

The others nodded. The choice of film was always a matter of lively discussion in their little group. As a rule, the host had the right to decide, which could be trying sometimes. It also led to them all seeing films they wouldn't have chosen otherwise, so the system worked as far as Leeland was concerned. They put their dirty dishes away, got bowls, which they filled with tiramisu and panna cotta, and then settled on the two couches to watch the dead come alive.

When the butterfly started flying through the strangely colored world of the *Corpse Bride*, Leeland leaned back and looked at his friends. Collin was staring at the screen with the rapt attention of a five-year-old, forming the words of the first song with his lips. Dean and Curtis were sitting next to each other, the box of tissues between them. Peyton was still pretending—and failing—to be insulted by the choice of film.

Leeland smiled. An evening with close friends, delicious food, and a damn good film, no matter what Peyton thought. At home his hot-as-fuck boyfriend was waiting. Life couldn't get much better.

AT ELEVEN thirty Leeland and Emilio said their goodbyes to Collin. Curtis had already left, taking Peyton with him. Dean was helping Collin with the kitchen, which meant loading the dishwasher in a manner that would later cause Martin to take all the dirty dishes out again and rearrange them in a "sensible fashion," as he liked to call it. Leeland had seen the same scene unfold every time Collin took charge of the dishwasher, and he wasn't entirely sure if the loopy artist wasn't doing it on purpose. Or perhaps there simply was an artistic side to arranging the cutlery in the dishwasher that eluded everybody except Collin. Then again, Dean was suspiciously eager to help Collin, and Leeland knew his friend well enough to see the potential entertainment Dean could get out of this. And Dean had lost the last traces of his innocence shortly after Richard introduced him to the world of BDSM. This was a mystery Leeland didn't feel the need to solve, at least not tonight.

He climbed behind the steering wheel of the Volvo he had borrowed from Jonathan while Emilio entered the passenger's side. Jonathan insisted on Leeland driving with a safe vehicle, which was cute in a very Neanderthal kind of way and also somehow patronizing since Jonathan's preferred method of transportation were his Harleys, which weren't necessarily known for their safety. On the other hand, it was nice to drive a car with heated seating, parking assist system, a very badass sound system, and all the other amenities money could buy and a boyfriend with his own garage could put into a vehicle. Leeland had come to love the automatically adjusting driver's seat and the massage function Jonathan had put in, which could be activated whenever the car stopped. Being stuck in traffic had never been so relaxing.

Emilio was staring out of the window, and Leeland realized he was even quieter than usual.

"Everything okay?" Leeland couldn't help but ask, even though he felt a bit nosy. He was almost sure Emilio would turn to him if he needed anything. Almost.

"Yes. It was a long day."

"Are you still upset about the food?"

Emilio shook his head. "No. I mean, yes, I am, but not in the way you think. It was my decision to eat it, and it was delicious." Emilio's hands wandered down to his crotch. "And soon I'm going to find out if it was worth it."

"If you'd wanted it to have been worth your while, you should have eaten the tiramisu as well. If punishment is a given, why not go all the way and indulge yourself fully?"

Emilio sighed. "You're probably right."

Leeland grinned. He sensed he wouldn't get anything out of Emilio tonight and wanted to lighten the mood. "I'm almost always right. Just don't ask Jonathan; he might have a different opinion. Speaking of which, there's something I wanted to ask you."

Leeland took Emilio's shy glance as his cue.

"Since I'm going to move in with Jonathan, I wanted to rent the apartment out. I'm a bit wary, though. You know, not all tenants are reliable, and after all the work Peyton put into making the apartment pretty, I'd hate to see it mistreated. Not to mention Peyton's reaction if anything happened to the kitchen or his precious dresser. I mean, you heard him in there." Leeland shuddered. "That's why I would rather have somebody live there who I already know."

Emilio didn't respond. Since it was too late to beat around the bush, Leeland went for the direct approach.

"I would appreciate it if you could move into my place, Emilio."

Emilio blushed so hard, Leeland could see the change of color in his cheeks even in the dim dashboard light. "That's very nice, Leeland, but I don't have the money. I can barely pay the rent for my one-room place."

Leeland shook his head. "I know that, Emilio. How much do you pay?"

"Six hundred."

"Then how about you cover the HOA fees for my apartment while I decide what to do with it?"

"Leeland! I can't do that. You could ask for at least two thousand for the place. Probably more now that Peyton is done with it."

Emilio was right, of course, but Leeland had different reasons for offering the apartment to him.

"It's not about the money, Emilio. I earn enough at Whisper, and Jonathan made it clear he won't take rent from me. I'm lucky. And I want others to be lucky as well. Renting the apartment to you is one way of paying the universe back, so to speak. Besides, that way I have somebody I trust living there."

Emilio was clearly flustered. "Are you sure?" He didn't sound as if he could believe somebody would actually be so kind to him, and it tore at Leeland's heart and hardened his resolve to have Emilio living at his place. The boy deserved some good things in his life after all the shit he'd been through. He reached over and patted Emilio's thigh in a reassuring manner. If only Emilio would realize that not all people were selfish, heartless bastards like his family and former friends.

"Absolutely. I don't want to embarrass you, but that place of yours…."

"I know. It's a dump." Emilio averted his eyes, and it didn't take a genius to know it was in shame. Leeland couldn't have that. He wanted Emilio to gain self-confidence, not lose it.

"Hey, you listen to me, Emilio. It's unbelievable what you have achieved all on your own. You worked very hard to be where you are now, with a place to call your own and a scholarship at Miami Dade. Don't let anybody take that away from you. I admire you for your strength—we all do, by the way—and because of that, I want to help you."

A smile blossomed on Emilio's face and lit it up. "Thank you, Leeland. Coming from you, it means a lot to me."

"Do we have a deal?"

"We have a deal."

Leeland grinned happily. Now all he had to do was tell Jonathan about the bargain he had made with Peyton—something he did not look forward to—and about his plans to let Emilio live in the apartment—which he was sure Jonathan would approve of.

All in all, life was good.

CHAPTER 4

Two weeks later

JONATHAN STOOD on the threshold to the living room of Leeland's apartment, admiring the view. Two perfect, taut asses were high in the air, occasionally wiggling when their owners swayed back or forth on their hands and knees. What he saw was so stunning, not even the constant bickering filling the air could dampen Jonathan's arousal.

"Why did you move that stupid shelf in the first place?" Dean sounded exasperated.

"I wanted to check for dust bunnies." Leeland's answer was petulant. Jonathan could practically see the pout, even though his boy's delectable back was to him.

"Leeland! This is your apartment we're talking about. There are no dust bunnies. If there ever have been any, they packed their little dust bags long ago and moved out to live with Peyton."

Dean was right, of course, Jonathan thought. Leeland was a clean freak.

"I just wanted to make sure. What would Emilio think if he came here and found dust behind the shelf?"

Dean sighed. "First of all, he probably wouldn't even look. That shelf is heavy, and not all of us are obsessed with cleaning." His ass wiggled enticingly as he shifted his weight to hold up a hand to keep Leeland from interfering. "And secondly, I think he'll be more upset about the TV not working."

"Maybe." Leeland sounded a bit meek. "So how do we fix this?"

"Well, all those plugs have to go somewhere, right? We just have to figure out where."

Leeland snorted. "Dean, the only thing I know about plugs and cables is that the one with the forky end goes into the socket. And last time I checked, you weren't much better."

"I'm not."

Jonathan watched as the two butts became very still, both men seemingly lost in thought. When Dean started talking again, he sounded as if he was testing a theory.

"We could ask somebody."

"And admit that we fucked up and are completely clueless? How long would Richard rib you about something like that? Because Jonathan wouldn't let go of it for *months*! He has the memory of an elephant."

Dean's ass swayed a bit as he shifted his weight more onto his knees. Jonathan had trouble keeping the laughter in. Of course his boy was right. He was going to have a lot of fun with this one.

"We could just… put the shelf back, you know."

Now it was Leeland's turn to shift around while he seemingly contemplated this idea.

"That would be cruel. Leaving Emilio to fend for himself. I mean, he does have Master Garrett, but he doesn't strike me as particularly—apt when it comes to electric appliances. Besides, we're not Doms. We don't do cruelty."

Jonathan decided it was time to make his presence known. As it was, his boy was already facing a punishment tonight. He cleared his throat. It was almost comical to watch as Dean and Leeland scrambled into upright positions, facing Jonathan with sheepish looks. Adorable blushes entered their cheeks, and the glances they exchanged made them look like very naughty boys who had been caught red-handed.

"Master Jonathan, what a nice surprise."

Dean tried for nonchalant and failed miserably. Leeland took a more direct approach, which turned Jonathan on even more.

"How much have you heard?"

Jonathan smiled evilly. "Enough to get you into trouble."

Leeland pouted, but Jonathan could tell from the gleam in his eyes how much the idea of a punishment appealed to him.

"Perhaps you could help us, Master Jonathan. We've run into a bit of trouble with the TV."

If there was a hint of challenge in Dean's voice, Jonathan decided to ignore it. He could always have a talk with Richard later.

"Let me take a look."

Jonathan went down on his knees to peek behind the shelf, where he was greeted by a nest of cables that reminded him of coiling snakes. He had set up his own sound system at home and was confident he could work it out. How difficult could it be to plug in some cables? He started fiddling with the black cords in an attempt to get them straight, which wasn't as easy as he had anticipated. The things acted as if they had a life of their own. Once he had all the cords lying in line, he examined them closely and felt his heart sinking. The system at home was color-coded, designed to be used by the clueless, as the nice geeky salesman had explained when Jonathan bought it. Leeland's TV and cables were obviously meant to be set up by pros, because they had no color codes. It was all black with funnily shaped plugs that looked more like something from *Star Trek* than appliances meant to be used by normal people for a simple sound system. Customizing a car or bike was easy compared to the dizzying amount of possibilities the plugs presented. There was no way he could know which cable went where. Jonathan felt sweat break out on his brow. He would never live this down. His mind went a mile a minute in an attempt to find a way to wriggle out of it but came up empty. Suddenly he heard Leeland's voice close to his ear, which reminded him that the two subs were probably watching him like hawks.

"Having trouble, Master?" The hint of amusement didn't escape Jonathan.

"Watch it, boy. This is more complicated than I thought. You have no color code!"

"I'm sorry. Next time I let Richard buy me a sound and TV system, I'm going to insist on having my cables in different colors."

Jonathan rose and smacked Leeland's ass. The boy winced.

"Ouch."

"You deserved that and you know it."

"Maybe. Fine, yes, I deserved it. Doesn't change the fact that it's still not working."

"Weell…." Dean glanced around the room, trying to look innocent. "Leeland and I may not do cruelty, but we have a Dom present now…."

Jonathan glared at him, and Dean had the decency to look embarrassed.

"Yes, I am a Dom. And, yes, Doms can be cruel when their subs deserve it. Right now I know of two who can look forward to some serious punishment. It also doesn't serve a Dom well to appear weak in front of subs in general. Which is why I'm going to prove my manliness and prowess by putting that shelf back where it was."

Jonathan was very proud of himself for delivering that speech without having his lips twitch once. As soon as he looked at his boy and Dean, though, who were trying their level best not to giggle, he lost it. They all started laughing so loud, they almost didn't hear the bell. Dean wiped tears from his eyes.

"That must be Richard with the van."

Richard had taken on the task of organizing two vans to transport Leeland's and Emilio's possessions to their respective new places. Jonathan went to open the door while Dean and Leeland started checking the packed cardboard boxes once more.

The man at the door was not Richard. He wore a beige T-shirt with the slogan *Happy Moving—You Move, We Do the Heavy Lifting*. It wasn't the most ingenious slogan ever but charming in its bluntness. Jonathan looked at the man. He already had an inkling where this was going.

"Yes?"

The man cleared his throat.

"Are you Mr. Leeland Drake?"

"No, I'm his partner, Jonathan. How can I help you?"

"We're here to move Mr. Drake to his new address. A Richard Miller hired us."

Jonathan frowned. "He was supposed to hire two vans, not a moving crew."

The man squirmed a bit. "He said he didn't do heavy lifting."

Jonathan snorted. "I can imagine. Come in."

When the man entered the living room where all the boxes were stacked, Dean and Leeland looked up in surprise. Jonathan grinned.

"This is…." He looked at the man expectantly.

"Oh, yes, sorry. I'm Bob. I'm in charge of your move."

Dean's eyes narrowed to slits.

"Let me guess, Richard hired you."

Bob avoided Dean's glare, obviously sensing that something wasn't right. For a sub, Dean could be quite intimidating if he wanted to. Jonathan had seen him develop this talent after he got Emily. If he remembered correctly, Leeland called it Dean's "dad glare."

"Yes?" Bob sounded hesitant, as if he seriously wished to be somewhere else. Jonathan could relate.

Before Dean could open his mouth, Richard entered the room. Jonathan remembered that he had left the door open, assuming the rest of the moving crew would come up. Dean looked at his master.

"You were supposed to hire a van, not a crew." He sounded almost accusing.

Richard shrugged. To Jonathan, he didn't look particularly repentant.

"Hiring a crew to do the moving was only slightly more expensive than just getting the vans, so I indulged."

"You just don't want to do any lifting!" There was a hint of laughter in Dean's voice now.

"I was put in charge of taking care of transportation, I took care of transportation. If you and Leeland failed to be specific, that's not my problem. Bob, do your thing."

"Of course, Mr. Miller." Bob clearly knew who was in charge. He left the apartment to instruct his crew. Richard pulled Dean into his arms.

"Admit it, love, it's much better this way. We can leave the boxes to Bob and his no doubt capable men and drive over to Jonathan's place, have a nice drink while we wait, and you and Leeland can prepare for when the boxes arrive."

"You, Master, are horribly well prepared." Dean grinned. "Must be why I love you so much."

Richard smacked Dean's backside. "I hope there's more reasons than just my ability to organize and delegate."

"I might come up with something on our way to Jonathan's."

Richard looked at Jonathan, who had slung his arm around Leeland's waist.

"Are you good to go?"

Jonathan nodded. He couldn't wait to get his boy into his lair, this time for good.

"Yeah, let's go."

They wanted to leave the house keys with Bob so he could close the apartment, but the man shook his head.

"The other crew at Mr. Vidal's place is almost done. We'll wait till they're here. That way the apartment isn't left unattended."

Jonathan smiled at the man. Bob had just earned himself a generous tip.

"Thank you, Bob."

He took Leeland's hand and led his boy to the elevator and out of the building. Richard and Dean had already climbed into Richard's Z8, ready to leave. Jonathan went to his Volvo, opened the passenger's side so Leeland could get seated, then rounded the car, climbed in, and started the engine.

"You and me, Leeland. I'm so happy."

Jonathan didn't know why he had said it, but the radiant smile on his boy's face told him it was good.

"Me, too, Jonathan. So happy."

"Okay, let's see what else Richard has paid for."

Leeland laughed. "You should have seen his face when Dean told him we wanted to do the move ourselves. He was downright horrified."

"Well, having Bob around does make things easier."

Having a moving crew was like shooting starlings with cannons. Emilio only had his clothing, a few books, some toiletries, and his battered old laptop to pack. And since Jonathan's apartment was already fully furnished, Leeland wasn't bringing any furniture except his favorite wing chair. The only heavy lifting they had to do were the boxes with his books and said chair.

Jonathan felt a cold shudder running down his spine when he remembered what else would come with Leeland—Peyton had already come by once to compare the blueprints of the apartment with the actual room situation. Just thinking about the adventurous gleam in the interior designer's eyes made Jonathan wince inwardly. There was no doubt, once Peyton was done with his apartment, he probably wouldn't recognize it anymore.

Jonathan sighed. Who was he kidding? As long as Leeland was happy, he didn't care about anything else. And Peyton was a genius.

It would just take time and money, two things Jonathan could spare. He looked over at his beautiful boy and thanked fate and whoever was in charge of the HEA of Doms and their subs for the gift they had bestowed on him.

CHAPTER 5

Three weeks later

LEELAND STOOD in the kitchen, preparing the salad that would go with the fish he was cooking for dinner. Settling in with Jonathan had been surprisingly easy, probably because he had already spent most of his time at the apartment even before the move. Emilio, too, was ecstatic about his new lodgings and, as it turned out, Curtis, who had helped Emilio settle in, was very good at hooking up entertainment systems. The man definitely had some hidden depths. The only downside at the moment was the construction going on in the apartment. Peyton had wasted no time turning the place into something "presentable," as he put it. Though Mike and Jeff—Peyton's business partners and contractors—did their best not to inconvenience Jonathan and Leeland, always working on one room only so they could close the door on the construction site, there were times when Leeland wished he had resisted Peyton more firmly, especially last week when Mike and Jeff had taken down two walls to make the living room bigger and create one generous guest room, sacrificing what Peyton called "the remnants of the Stone Age of interior design," meaning lots of smaller rooms instead of big open spaces. Those "remnants" had turned the entire apartment into a dusty hell, and it had taken Leeland three days of frantic cleaning until everything was back to normal. Or as normal as it could be till all the renovations were done. When he had complained to Peyton about the dirt, the man just mumbled something about necessary sacrifices and how nobody seemed to be able to appreciate his genius.

The workers were gone for the day, which left Leeland alone to do the cooking. He was just slicing the tomatoes when his cell rang. Leeland furrowed his brow at the caller ID.

"Uncle Misaki?"

"Hello, Leeland. It's good to hear your voice."

"Yes, it is, Uncle." Misaki Aoki was not really Leeland's uncle. When Routa Hashimoto, Leeland's father, had fallen in love with an American woman and followed her to the States, his childhood friend Misaki was the only one of his old circle of friends and family who didn't shun him for breaking with tradition. Three years after Routa had married Layla Drake and taken on her last name, Misaki couldn't stand the restrictions of rural Japanese society anymore and followed his friend into the land of endless opportunities. The men maintained their close friendship, and when Leeland was born, Misaki became his godfather. He was also the man who had helped train Leeland in several martial arts. They still kept in touch, mainly at family gatherings, though it was unusual for Misaki to just call him. The man was incredibly busy with running his MMA gym.

"To what do I owe the pleasure of talking to you?"

As a Japanese man, Misaki would dance around the reason for his call endlessly, as Leeland knew only too well. The only way to get the information quickly was to ask directly, even though it wasn't considered polite, at least in Japan. Leeland was too American to care, and he already sensed this wasn't a courtesy call.

"Well, since you're asking so directly…." There was a hint of reproach in Misaki's voice, paired with a dash of amusement. He had lived in the country long enough and been around enough MMA fighters not to be offended by the "American bluntness," as he called it, that Leeland had inherited from his mother.

"Yes, I am asking directly." Leeland smiled at the salad in front of him.

"I have to ask a favor of you, Lee-kun. A big favor."

Leeland felt a chill creeping up his spine. This sounded ominous.

"What's wrong, *Ojisan?*" Automatically, Leeland fell back on the Japanese form to address his uncle.

"As you know, I've started a charity, Hinode."

Leeland nodded, even though Misaki couldn't see it. He loved the project that offered children without money the opportunity to train at Misaki's gym, thus keeping them off the streets and out of trouble. His parents, both cops, helped however they could.

"Are there problems with the project?"

"No, but however."

Leeland took a deep breath. "Ojisan, please tell me what's going on."

His uncle sighed. Even though he couldn't see him, Leeland could practically feel his oji squirming.

"About six months ago, I got an offer that allowed me to expand the project. A European company that produces an energy drink called Smash! wants in to the US market. They're looking to maintain a certain image and approached me, asking if I could train somebody to send to official fights with the UFC. I had a promising candidate I wanted to place there, and with the financial backing from Smash! everything was great until two days ago. My man was in a car accident. His leg is broken, and as you can imagine, he's out for this season. Perhaps even for the next, depending on how the healing and rehab go. The contract with the UFC is already signed, but they're willing to accept a substitute. Smash! has already set up everything for this season, up to a point where withdrawing is going to cost them more money than staying on with a candidate who isn't likely to win." Misaki paused, and Leeland knew what was coming next. "Which brings me to you."

"You want me to compete?" Leeland couldn't believe it.

"I know I'm asking a lot. And you don't have to. Just think about it, please. I need the money for the project, and I can't say for sure if the people from Smash! will keep me on if I can't produce a substitute. They want an in with the UFC, and they want it immediately."

Talk about putting the pressure on. Leeland knew Misaki wasn't cornering him intentionally, but he sure made saying no difficult. While he was still trying to wrap his head around the proposal his uncle had just made, Leeland remembered something important.

"I'm out and proud, Ojisan. Last time I checked, the MMA world wasn't very accepting of gays, and I'm pretty sure that hasn't changed, no matter what Dana White says in front of the cameras. There's still no gay man out in the UFC, and you and I both know why. I'm not going back into the closet, not even for you. I don't think I could at this point. Given my lifestyle, somebody would find out. Does your sponsor know you're asking a gay man?"

Misaki sighed again, this time even more emphatically.

"Yes. As I said, they're between a rock and a hard place, and as Samantha Jones, the PR lady for Smash! has so eloquently put it, there's nothing worse than no PR. Sponsoring a gay fighter may not have been their original plan, but it will definitely garner them a lot of attention."

"You mean they want to turn me into a gay poster boy?" Leeland didn't even try to keep the anger from his voice. If there was one thing he despised even more than hiding who he was, it was being used for who he was. Why couldn't people just let him be?

"No, of course not. You should know me better, Lee-kun. I already told Samantha you aren't happy with publicity, which in turn made her unhappy. We finally agreed on not hiding the gay angle but not promoting it either. Depending on how successful you are, people will start digging regardless, but with any luck they will make their big finds toward the end of the season."

"Fine. So I may or may not become the first out gay UFC fighter. How wonderful." Leeland felt so rattled, he didn't even try to keep the sarcasm out of his voice, even though he usually wasn't that disrespectful toward his uncle. That Misaki let it slide without comment only upset Leeland more, because it showed how desperate he had to be. "What about my studies? I only have one year left, and I can't just take a leave of absence."

Misaki sounded a bit guilty when he answered. "I already checked with Miami Dade. The prospect of having a professional MMA athlete to add to their list of students was enough to make them very accommodating. They're going to keep your scholarship on hold, and Smash! will pay you for the time you can't study so you don't lose any money over this."

Leeland was stunned. He didn't know if he should be annoyed or amused and decided to postpone his reaction.

"You seem to be awfully sure I'm going to do this."

"To be honest, yes. You know I wouldn't be asking this of you if I had another choice, but I don't. Plus you're an incredibly talented fighter, you already have experience competing, and I know you still train regularly. Getting you into shape for competing may be a challenge depending on how soon your first fight is scheduled, but

I'm convinced we can do it. I even see a chance for you winning some of the matches."

Leeland snorted. "Flattery won't get you my cooperation, Ojisan. I'm not going to lie to you, I'm tempted. But I have to talk to Jonathan first. We're living together now, and he gets a say in this. Something as big as this is going to affect our lives deeply, and I want him to know what he would be getting into and to make an educated decision. I'm going to talk to him tonight and call you back tomorrow. That's all I can promise right now."

"And it's more than you have to, Lee-kun. Thank you." Misaki ended the call, and the genuine relief in his uncle's voice tore at Leeland's heart. Misaki was family, just like his parents and Jonathan and Dean and all the other men at Whisper he had formed friendships with. Not helping the man who had helped raise him went against everything Leeland had learned to believe in. It was true, though, that going pro, even if it was just for one season and not with the goal to win anything—something that didn't sit well with Leeland either; when he fought, he fought to win—would change their life dramatically. Leeland only hoped he would be able to explain matters to Jonathan in a way that enabled his master to make an informed decision.

Saddened, Leeland looked at the sauce simmering on the stove. A creamy goodness like this would be just one of the many things he would have to relinquish if he agreed to help his uncle.

CHAPTER 6

JONATHAN ENTERED the apartment and knew immediately something was wrong. Where he was usually greeted by an atmosphere of tranquility, he now felt nervous energy. Leeland approached him down the hall from where the kitchen was located, looking jumpy and unhappy.

"Boy." Jonathan simply opened his arms, allowing Leeland to throw himself into his embrace. Because Leeland was so self-reliant, such displays of vulnerability rarely happened. Jonathan wondered what had his boy so upset.

"Jonathan." Leeland sounded both relieved and agitated, which didn't make sense to Jonathan.

"What's happened? Is it something with your friends? Or at college?"

Leeland drew back in Jonathan's arms, looking as if the weight of the world was on his shoulders.

"No. My friends are fine, and college is going smoothly. I'm sorry if I worried you. The last hour has been weird." Leeland took Jonathan's hand and led him to the kitchen, where the dinner table was already set. Jonathan let himself be guided toward one of the chairs, sat down, and accepted the water Leeland poured from a glass carafe. While Leeland busied himself with mixing tagliatelle—at least Jonathan thought that was what these noodles were called; to him it was all just delicious carbohydrates in a pleasing form—with a sauce that smelled divine, Jonathan tried to gauge his boy's mood. Leeland didn't seem angry. For that his movements were still too fluid. He wasn't sad either. No tears, no sniffling, and, most importantly, no empty ice-cream containers and chocolate wrappings littering the kitchen. Leeland just seemed—restless. Like something was eating at him from the inside. Jonathan was fairly sure it didn't have to do with their relationship either. They were solid and practiced a firm policy of openness. Hiding things was a bad idea in any relationship, but even more so in one that involved BDSM.

Before he got together with Leeland, Jonathan had envied couples like Richard and Dean from a safe distance, sticking to a rigorous "spank them, then leave them" rule, mostly because the parameters during a single encounter could be more easily controlled than the ones in a steady relationship. In that regard Jonathan was a typical Dom, always wanting to be in absolute control. Then he had fallen in love with Leeland and everything changed. It was just like Richard had told him once—the scenes got more intense, even small gestures took on a different, deeper meaning, and the chances to fuck up multiplied. But so did the joy, the lust, the emotions. When you were in love, everything was more.

It had taken Jonathan some time to adapt to the intensity Leeland brought into his life, and sometimes it had scared the shit out of him, but now he didn't want to miss even one second. He loved being the person Leeland turned to when he needed help, being his rock, his anchor. Seeing his boy so agitated woke Jonathan's most primal urges to protect and shelter. If it weren't for the irrational need to spill somebody's blood, those feelings wouldn't be too bad. After all, they showed how deeply he cared for his boy.

Leeland was apparently done mixing the noodles and the sauce, brought the pot over to the table, and served first Jonathan, then himself.

"Smells amazing, honey."

Leeland smiled weakly. "*Tagliatelle al salmone.* I know you like fish."

Jonathan reached out to stroke Leeland's cheek, full of love.

"Thank you. I appreciate it. Now, are you going to tell me what has you so upset, or should we eat first?"

Leeland glanced at his plate, then back to Jonathan.

"We eat first."

Jonathan nodded in agreement. He had a suspicion they wouldn't have much of an appetite once Leeland spilled the beans about what had him so stressed. They ate in peaceful silence, neither of them wanting to make small talk while there was clearly such an elephant lurking in the room, even though Jonathan was itching to find out the shape and size of said elephant. Once they were finished with their meal, Jonathan cleared the table, putting the plates in the dishwasher before he took Leeland's hand and led him to the living room, where they settled on the dark green leather couch. Leeland snuggled in Jonathan's lap. Jonathan pressed a kiss to Leeland's forehead.

"Time to talk, boy."

Leeland sat up a bit straighter so he could look Jonathan in the eyes.

"Uncle Misaki called today."

Jonathan furrowed his brows. He had met Leeland's family only a handful of times in the almost twelve months since they'd started dating. Misaki was an important part of Leeland's life, even though they didn't talk that regularly. From what Jonathan understood, the man had taught Leeland martial arts and had been—and still was—a great influence on his life.

"Is he okay?"

"Yes and no. He's having some trouble and wants me to go pro in the UFC for a year."

Jonathan hadn't seen that one coming.

"Why would he want you to do that?"

Leeland sighed. "You know my uncle's charity, Hinode, where he helps troubled kids. He has found a European sponsor for it who is willing to donate quite a lot of money. In exchange, they wanted Ojisan to train an athlete for the UFC through whom they could promote their energy drink. Said athlete was in a car accident some days ago, and now my ojisan needs a replacement. Apparently the UFC is willing to change the contract so somebody else can fight for my ojisan's gym."

"And you're his first choice?" Jonathan didn't mean to be derogatory, and Leeland didn't seem to take his words the wrong way.

"Nobody was more surprised than me. It's been almost two years since I last competed, and that was not in MMA, but in jiu-jitsu, karate, and judo. I wanted to concentrate on my studies once I had finally found the perfect major."

Jonathan knew this was a bit of a sore subject for Leeland. He had started out with a different major, history of art, only to realize that he felt more comfortable with graphic design. If they had already dated back when Leeland made the switch, Jonathan would have reassured his boy that it was absolutely fine to change one's mind about something, but as it was, Leeland had gone through the strain of deciding to change his major and then actually doing it, alone. In an effort to take Leeland's mind off that time in his life, Jonathan focused on the first part of his explanation.

"How successful were you?" Jonathan was curious. He liked that Leeland could take care of himself and was fascinated by all the different martial arts his boy had mastered, but Leeland never talked about tournaments or championships. Jonathan knew it had more to do with Leeland's modesty and nothing with shutting Jonathan out, so he wasn't angry. As if to confirm his assumptions, Leeland squirmed uncomfortably in Jonathan's lap.

"Three times national champion in both judo and jiu-jitsu. One time national champion in karate, junior league, and second in the young adult category."

"Wow." Jonathan was surprised. That was even more impressive than he had assumed. He briefly wondered where Leeland kept all the trophies. Probably stashed away in his parents' attic. The whole family wasn't one for bragging. "I can see why he would want you."

Leeland shook his head. "As I said, it's almost two years since I last competed. I stay in shape, and I know my moves, but I guess the main reason is because he wants somebody he knows. Starting all over with a new athlete he hasn't formed himself would be stressful, especially on such short notice. If he had a suitable candidate in his gym, he wouldn't have contacted me."

Sensing his boy's distress, Jonathan started drawing soothing circles on Leeland's rigid back. "So what's the issue? I know you want to help your uncle, but you also seem reluctant at the same time. Do you want to explain your dilemma to me?"

For a moment Leeland didn't say anything. If he hadn't known his lover so well, Jonathan might have started to worry, but he knew Leeland was merely trying to get his thoughts in order. Given the enormity of Misaki's proposal, Jonathan could see how that might be difficult for Leeland.

"You're right. I do want to help my ojisan. He's family, after all. But so are you and agreeing to Ojisan's proposal is going to affect you a lot. Our life." Leeland drew a deep breath. "And I'm not sure if I want that."

"Explain." Against his will, Jonathan felt a little tense. If he was honest, he hadn't thought about the impact such a decision would have on him or their relationship. He had thought of it as Leeland's problem, with which he would help him deal. Since Leeland was that worried, it had to be bigger than he initially imagined.

"First of all, I'd have to take a leave of absence from college. Apparently that won't be a problem. Ojisan has already talked to them, and they're delighted to grant me a leave as long as they can add my name to the list of the college's active athletes."

"Wasn't that a bit presumptuous?"

Leeland shrugged. "Ojisan knows me. He wanted to eliminate as many objections I might have as possible. Anyway, I'd lose a year. The sponsor is going to pay me, though, so it wouldn't be a financial loss. Then there's the gay angle. There's no openly out male fighter in the UFC, and MMA in general is not exactly a stronghold of gay rights and open-mindedness, even though they are better than the NFL, and that's not a compliment for the UFC, as you well know."

Jonathan snorted. Which sport, aside from dressage and maybe figure skating, was truly open to the concept of gay athletes? Though he had to admit the NHL was making quite an effort to encourage people from the LGBTQ spectrum.

"I told Ojisan I wouldn't hide who I am, and he and the sponsor both are fine with that. As long as we don't advertise it—which I don't plan on doing—there shouldn't be any problems, though that depends on how well I do. The more matches I win, the more attention I will get from the media. Another thing I don't fancy, and not just because of the gay issue."

"Okay. So college seems to be cleared. The media exposure is tied to a lot of what-ifs, which leads me to believe there's more." Jonathan was proud of his sober analysis.

Leeland took Jonathan's fingers and started playing with them. "You're right. Those are only the small problems." He took a deep breath. "If I agree, I won't just show up for the fights and hope for the best, even though the sponsor would be fine with it, but that's not who I am. If I compete, I compete to win. I'd have to train, and since there's not much time, I'd have to train hard. We're talking a minimum of six hours a day, accompanied by a strict diet to get into perfect shape. Ojisan hasn't told me in which weight class he wants to nominate me, but depending on that, I have to either gain muscle mass or lose weight. *Tagliatelle al salmone* will become a distant wet dream for me."

Leeland leaned back a bit, and Jonathan could see a hint of sadness in his eyes.

"I will be sore and covered in bruises all the time, and not from doing a scene. Most days I'll be too tired to do more than fall headfirst into bed. The BDSM part of our relationship would be on hold, with only a few small scenes when I'm not completely exhausted. And that is definitely a part of our life that we would have to keep hidden. It's one thing to be an out athlete, but being an out athlete with a kink—that's just not worth the hate we're going to get."

A single tear slipped down Leeland's left cheek, telling louder than his agitated speech how much this upset him. Jonathan caught the tear, trying to understand his own feelings. He could see where this was going and why Leeland was so unhappy.

"You're afraid this will impact our relationship negatively."

Leeland nodded. Jonathan leaned back on the couch, dragging Leeland with him until their upper bodies were snuggled closely together. It was a legitimate fear. The core of their relationship was BDSM. They both needed the kink in their lives to feel complete. When he was a young man, admitting his cravings to himself had been hard enough for Jonathan. Suppressing them now, even if it was only for a short time and for the man he loved, wasn't a happy thought. Judging from the slight trembling in Leeland's body, his boy's mind went along the same lines. This was not a decision that could be rushed.

"Are there any other catches?"

Leeland shook his head. His voice sounded a bit muffled when he tried to speak into Jonathan's pecs.

"No. I don't think we need more of them."

"You're right about that, boy." Jonathan started stroking Leeland's back. "Here is what we do, honey. We think about this thoroughly and discuss it tomorrow, when we've had time to digest it.

And because we both can do with a bit of a distraction, we're going to do a little scene now. Okay?"

Leeland's answer was a heartfelt "Yes."

Jonathan helped his boy to sit up on his lap. He scrutinized Leeland for a moment, slipping into his Dom mindset. Judging from the way Leeland's entire body relaxed, he was doing the same, embracing his submission, putting his trust in his Dom. Once both their breathing had evened out and synchronized, Jonathan put Leeland on his feet.

"Go to the bedroom. Strip and assume the presentation position. We're on high protocol."

"Yes, Master." Leeland turned and went to their bedroom.

Jonathan exhaled, glad they were able to fall into their established routine so quickly. It was the strong foundation on which their relationship was built. What would happen if they lost that foundation, no matter how temporarily, he didn't want to imagine.

CHAPTER 7

LEELAND HURRIED to the bedroom and stripped quickly. Explaining the consequences of going along with Misaki's proposal had intensified his doubts and heightened his fear of losing Jonathan. It had taken Leeland too long to find the perfect man to risk scaring him off now. He didn't want to disappoint his ojisan either. The dilemma had his thoughts tumbling like marbles falling from a bag to the floor.

Inhaling deeply, Leeland knelt on the small carpet in bright orange and yellow, a gift from Collin that made Peyton roll his eyes every time he saw it. Since he was doing the redecorating, that happened regularly. Leeland suspected that deep down, Peyton was a masochist who wanted to torture himself with the sight of the monstrosity, as he called it. It certainly lit up the man cave Jonathan called his bedroom, with its imposing four-poster king-size bed in a polished dark wood Leeland couldn't recall the name of. The walls were painted white, which only served to accentuate the black wooden ceiling and the heavy antique vanity dresser that had given Peyton a migraine on his first inspection. The small carpet was one of Collin's first attempts at weaving, and even though it certainly didn't fit in the bedroom—or any other room in Jonathan's apartment, come to think of it—it was definitely interesting, and not in a bad way. Leeland was almost sure Jonathan kept the carpet simply to annoy Peyton. And because he couldn't deal with Collin's kicked-puppy look should he get rid of it.

The act of kneeling down and getting into position helped Leeland focus. He could feel his stumbling thoughts calming as he sank deeper into his subspace. Hearing the command from Jonathan in the living room had started this process, and Leeland knew at the end of tonight's scene he would find serenity. Jonathan was good like that.

A soft rustling at the door alerted Leeland to the presence of his master. He forced his body to be completely still, to just be there for the man he loved. Jonathan entered the room and halted right behind Leeland. Because Leeland was facing the bed, away from the door, he had to rely on his hearing to place Jonathan. His heart hammered away in his chest as he sensed Jonathan's considerable bulk behind him. All his instincts screamed at him to turn around, to kick out to bring Jonathan down and then neutralize him, just like his parents and Uncle Misaki had taught him to do. The only reason he didn't follow this urge was the absolute trust he had in Jonathan. He was the first Dom Leeland allowed behind his back without a mirror to control what was happening.

"Nice position, boy. I love your posture."

The warm voice washed over Leeland, lulled his survival instincts to sleep, assured the beast inside him that this, *this* was the man they trusted. The man who made them feel loved and pampered and sheltered, even when he hurt them.

"Thank you, Master."

Unlike many Doms, Jonathan rarely forbade Leeland to speak. They both relied heavily on verbal communication to get their needs and wishes across. For them it was an additional way of forming a connection during the scene, and Leeland loved it.

Jonathan circled him once before he stopped between Leeland and the bed. His voice was already rugged, barely more than a harsh whisper, tinted with arousal.

"Tonight I'm not going to hurt you, boy. Tonight I'm going to make you lose your fucking mind. I will drive you to the point where you only need me, where all you can think about is how to get my cock in your ass so you can finally find release. I'll have you begging and whimpering and groaning my name, and when you think you can't take it anymore, I'll let you come."

Leeland didn't even try to suppress his needy whimper. He loved it when Jonathan talked dirty to him, when he described what he was going to do to Leeland. The words had his cock twitching, leaking precum in a steady stream.

Seemingly satisfied with this response, Jonathan stepped aside.

"Get up and lie down on the bed, on your back. Grab the headboard and don't let go, no matter what happens. Spread your legs."

Gracefully, Leeland rose from the floor to do as he was told. Once he was in position, Jonathan took what seemed an eternity to scrutinize him. Under the hot stare, Leeland felt his cock hardening until it was close to being painful. Small droplets of sweat started forming on his forehead, in the valley of his breastbone, and in the juncture where his thighs met his groin. Since Jonathan hadn't told him otherwise, Leeland looked directly at his handsome Dom, the sight of all those muscles beneath the clothes giving him a feeling of security.

Jonathan met his heated gaze, and for a moment they simply held eye contact. Then, with a lazy, seductive smile, Jonathan grabbed the hem of his T-shirt and took it off. Leeland felt drool forming in his mouth. With a knowing smirk, Jonathan started unbuttoning his trousers, directly in Leeland's line of sight. As always, Jonathan had gone commando, and the sight of that beautiful, large cock slowly rising from between the gaping fly had Leeland squirming.

It was almost ridiculous how turned on he was after a bit of dirty talk and a flash of cock. But Jonathan did that to him. Only Jonathan.

His master's hard shaft sprang free, pointing hungrily at Leeland as if seeking its target. With surprising grace for a man of his height and muscle mass, Jonathan turned around. Leeland's cock was slapping against his stomach with every labored breath he took while his Dom slowly exposed his fine, hard ass.

"Master, please!"

A low chuckle came from where Jonathan was now stepping out of his trousers.

"I haven't even started taking care of you, and you're already begging? Where's your endurance, boy?"

"Evaporated in the hotness of your ass."

That earned Leeland a guffaw. Not many Doms put up with a sub using strong language and being cheeky. Jonathan loved it. Another reason why he was so damn perfect for Leeland, who couldn't control his verbal output on a good day.

Jonathan was now completely naked. He positioned himself between Leeland's stretched legs, stroking his own shaft lazily while he looked at Leeland with a predatory gleam in his eyes.

"This is going to be so good, boy. So good."

Leeland nodded, too distracted by the sight of Jonathan's hand pumping his shaft to form syllables, let alone coherent sentences. Jonathan stopped the stroking. His fingertips grazed over Leeland's toes, along the ridges of his feet and up to his knees. Then Jonathan bent to the right, lifted Leeland's left leg straight in the air, and started licking the crease in the back of his knee.

Leeland almost came on the spot. His fingers tightened on the headboard while Jonathan kept on teasing one of his most erogenous zones. When Leeland thought he couldn't take it anymore, his master turned left to give his other knee the same attention. By the time Jonathan put Leeland's right leg down and his hands resumed their journey upward, Leeland was a panting, moaning mess of oversensitized nerve endings and pure need.

Jonathan proved just how cruel he could be by not touching Leeland's cock and balls at all. Instead he let his palms run over the smooth skin on Leeland's stomach, which caused Leeland to arch his spine.

Jonathan chuckled. "So hot for me, boy. You're good."

"Then let me come?"

Leeland figured it was worth a try. Jonathan didn't answer. He bent down to take one of Leeland's nipples in his mouth, and in a way, that told Leeland all he needed to know. His suffering wasn't over yet. After Jonathan had teased his nipples until they were hard little kernels, he finally, finally allowed his body to touch Leeland's. Their cocks slid against each other while Jonathan started kissing him.

Just when Leeland thought he couldn't take it anymore, Jonathan stopped. He caught Jonathan's heated gaze, and what he saw there made Leeland shiver in anticipation.

"If you don't like what I'm going to do, you tap me on the head three times. Got it?"

Nervously Leeland wetted his lips. He knew where this was going. Excitement and dread warred inside of him. Jonathan must have seen his inner conflict, because he brushed his lips over Leeland's nose.

"Just a little bit, honey. I swear, I'll stop the moment you tap me."

Leeland felt the sudden urge to placate Jonathan. This wasn't about him trusting Jonathan.

"I trust you. I'm just not sure if I trust myself."

"You're the one in control, Leeland. Always."

Leeland felt tears gathering in the corner of his eyes. Jonathan knew him so well.

"Thank you. I love you."

"And I love you, boy. Now, where was I? Ah yes, driving you crazy."

Jonathan started kissing him again, and Leeland felt the tension in his body melting. And when his master shuffled a bit sideways and started stroking his shaft with long, sure movements, Leeland almost forgot what was still to come.

Until Jonathan's other hand clamped down on his mouth. With his thumb and forefinger, Jonathan pinched Leeland's nose, literally taking his breath away. Leeland shuddered. The dueling sensations of panic at not being able to breath and of pure lust radiating from his cock were almost too much. The survival instincts his parents had honed and trained screamed at him to take Jonathan down, to act against the threat. His body, though, loved what was happening, loved the hormones flooding his system, the mixture of pain and pleasure as his lungs started to burn. He could end this anytime, an inner voice reminded him. He wasn't bound. It was his decision. His alone.

Jonathan let go of his nose, and Leeland gulped in huge lungfuls of air. All the time, Jonathan never stopped stroking Leeland's cock, winding up his need to come. Leeland didn't know what to think. Breath play had always been one of his hard limits. There was no Dom he trusted enough to control his breathing—until he met Jonathan. When they set up their contract and talked about limits, breath play had come up. It was something Jonathan wanted to try. Nevertheless he'd been willing to put it on the list of hard limits when Leeland insisted. After the first seven months together, Leeland had found he wasn't as averse to the idea as he had initially been. He and Jonathan talked it over and agreed to move it to the soft limits. From then on, Jonathan started including bits of breath play here and there. It was never at the core of a scene, and never when Leeland was bound. It gave him a chance to get used to the idea of Jonathan controlling his breathing, of surrendering to him in this new way. And Leeland found he liked it. That didn't mean he was totally relaxed, though.

Now Jonathan smiled down at him.

"My brave boy. I know how hard this is for you. You make me proud."

The words helped Leeland to relax even more. When Jonathan's finger pinched his nose again, Leeland kept their gazes locked, reveling again in the heady mixture of pain and pleasure Jonathan gave him. He felt his orgasm approaching fast but didn't want it to end. As if he had read his mind—perhaps he'd seen it in Leeland's eyes, Leeland couldn't tell—Jonathan took his hand away from Leeland's mouth and nose.

"Want to be inside you when you come, boy."

"Yes, please, Master. Please!"

Grinning, Jonathan reached for the lube on the nightstand. Leeland hadn't even realized it was there when they started the scene. Watching his Dom slick up his heavy, fat shaft had Leeland's hole twitching. He couldn't wait to feel the thick cock in his ass. When Jonathan finished lubing himself, he squirted a generous amount on his fingers. The predatory gleam in his eyes intensified when he breached Leeland's hole with his forefinger.

Leeland gasped and lifted his hips invitingly. He loved it when Jonathan prepared him. A second finger joined the first, quickly followed by a third. Leeland was so turned on, his hole accepted the intrusion willingly. But no matter how enthusiastic Leeland was, Jonathan still took his time loosening him properly, another reason why Leeland loved the man so much. Then after what felt like an eternity, Jonathan took his fingers out and positioned his cock on Leeland's hole. With one swift thrust, Leeland felt him entering and almost came on the spot because it was so good.

"God, boy, you're so tight. So hot. Gonna fuck you hard."

Leeland panted. His own cock was so hard, he thought it would explode any minute.

"Yes, please, Jonathan. Do me hard. Fuck me."

Grunting, Jonathan obliged. Usually he would start with a gentle rhythm to rev them both up, but not tonight. Tonight they were already too close. Leeland could see it in the way the vein on Jonathan's temple throbbed and how he clenched his teeth every time he rammed deep into Leeland's body.

Leeland felt the familiar tingling in his balls. With a cry he let go of the headboard and slung his arms around Jonathan's neck. Jonathan's grip on him tightened in return, and after two more powerful thrusts, they both came. Leeland felt Jonathan's cock twitch inside his body, the hotness of his seed coating his insides. His own cum acted as an adhesive between their upper bodies, making them slick and sticky at the same time. Jonathan fell down on his side, never letting go of Leeland. Snuggled closely, they slowly came down from the incredible high they had just shared. Leeland pressed lazy kisses on the place where his mouth rested against Jonathan's sweat-slick skin.

"Mmm. Salty Master. My favorite."

Jonathan pinched his ass. "Brat."

"Yes. Your brat."

"Mine."

Leeland must have dozed off after that, because the next thing he knew was the feeling of a warm, wet washcloth on his skin when Jonathan swiped the drying cum from his body. When he was done, he threw the washcloth in the direction of the bathroom before climbing into the bed again. He spooned Leeland from behind, which was Leeland's favorite way of falling asleep.

"Go back to sleep, honey. We'll talk tomorrow. I love you."

"Love you too. So much."

Leeland closed his eyes.

"So, HAVE you decided?" The next morning they were sitting in the kitchen, each with a cup of coffee. Jonathan looked at Leeland with what Leeland secretly called his "serious businessman disguise" look.

"Yes." Leeland took a deep breath. "Uncle Misaki is family, and family helps each other, so I'm inclined to do it. It's only for a limited time, and I'm young enough that losing a year in college isn't a catastrophe—especially since the costs are covered."

Leeland hesitated. He saw Jonathan lifting one of his eyebrows.

"I sense a 'but' coming."

"Not a 'but' per se. More of a caveat." Leeland met Jonathan's gaze full-on, hoping his lover could see how serious he was. "If you're opposed to the idea, I won't do it. Our relationship is too important to me. And there will be pressure, no doubt."

Again, one of Jonathan's eyebrows lifted.

"Do you think I wouldn't be able to deal with it?"

There was no malice in Jonathan's voice, which told Leeland that he was genuinely interested in the answer.

"To be honest, I don't know. We both know my trust in you when it comes to scenes is absolute. You're a strong, reliable, levelheaded man with a great ass."

The last Leeland said to lighten the mood, though it was true. Jonathan's ass was a piece of art as far as Leeland was concerned.

A smile appeared on Jonathan's lips. "I hope there's more to me than just my ass…."

Leeland gazed at his master appreciatively. "A lot more…."

Jonathan palmed his crotch in a very obvious gesture before he turned serious again.

"I understand, Leeland, and I can see where you're coming from. We both know I'm a novice when it comes to relationships. You're the first man I ever considered dating and—obviously—the first I've moved in with. I'm so new to being with somebody for more than just scenes and sex, I won't even try and pretend to know how much pressure we can handle. I also won't lie to both of us by saying everything will be fine."

Jonathan took a sip of his coffee. Leeland watched, mesmerized, not knowing what held his interest more—the enticing up and down of Jonathan's Adam's apple or his words. Jonathan White was more a man of action than discussing his feelings. That he had so much to say on this topic showed how important their life together was for him and how much thought he had put into this. Leeland felt his heart flutter at this unconventional, yet deeply moving, declaration of love. Jonathan went on.

"There are a few things I do know, though."

He looked directly at Leeland, a bright smile softening his features.

"I love you. I love us. You make me want to be a better man, and I don't care if it sounds cheesy. We are a solid unit, and we can trust each other." His smile took on a predatory quality. "As we saw last night."

Leeland blushed and felt his cock reacting to Jonathan's suggestive tone.

"I plan on spending the rest of my life with you, honey. though I didn't want to spring it on you like this." Now it was Jonathan who blushed.

Leeland melted. "That's a good thing, because I don't intend to ever let you go."

"Perfect. Where was I? Oh, yes. Staying with you forever. We both know life is not always roses and sunshine. There will be challenges, and I want to face them with you by my side. So let this be our first test. One we take on knowingly."

Leeland got up from his chair, rounded the table, and sat down on Jonathan's lap, slinging his arms around his master's neck.

"I love you so much. Thank you."

Jonathan embraced him, and Leeland felt the familiar, soothing warmth of his Dom seep into his body.

"I love you, Leeland. Now go and call your oji."

CHAPTER 8

ONLY TWO hours after Jonathan had listened to Leeland's conversation with his uncle on the phone, he was standing in Misaki's slightly run-down gym in Little Havana, watching while his boy fought in the ring against one of Misaki's trainers and business partner, an African American named Greg Smith. The gym was nothing like the polished establishment owned by Garrett Kiernan, another Dom at Whisper, where Jonathan went to keep his body in shape, but it had a certain raggedy charm that appealed to his inner animal. It was the kind of gym where he could imagine the members of *Fight Club* doing their training, a place that smelled of sweat and blood and testosterone, with a dash of mold from the aged building underneath. There were no mirrors, and the equipment, such as barbells, pressing benches, and punching bags, looked worn from having been used for too long. Nevertheless, the gym wasn't seedy. It was obviously well cared for and reflected its owner.

Greg, Leeland's opponent in this fight, appeared to be well into his thirties, was packed with muscle, and at least two heads taller than Leeland. Jonathan was surprised to see how tamely Leeland fought against Greg, which woke in Jonathan the silly urge to defend his boy.

"He's not usually that timid."

Misaki, whose graying hair gleamed silver in the sunlight filtering through the skylight, didn't take his dark eyes off the two fighters when he answered Jonathan.

"I hope not. Otherwise it could get him killed. But Greg has a few black belts, just like Leeland. He's also taller, which means he has a wider range, and he has at least thirty pounds of muscle on Leeland, if I had to make a guess. One well-aimed punch, and Leeland is out like a light because Greg produces a lot more force. So he has to stay defensive and wait for his chance. My godson is smart. He has already figured out Greg's weakness."

Pride was evident in Misaki's voice. Out of the corner of his eye, Jonathan watched Misaki. Even though the man was already sixty-five, he still packed a lot of muscle, and the skin on his face showed only few wrinkles. Had it not been for the strands of silver-white hair, Misaki could have passed for being in his late forties. During the few times they had met, Jonathan had found Misaki to be a pleasant, very polite man who loved his godson as if he were his own. Now, in his gym, on his home turf, so to speak, Misaki seemed to be more alert, sharper around the edges, though Jonathan wasn't sure if this was his imagination playing tricks on him. Things had definitely progressed quickly since this morning, and he felt a little out of his depth. He must have somehow telegraphed his confusion, because Misaki started talking again, addressing at least one of his unspoken questions.

"Greg was in an accident a couple of years ago. Since then, his left knee hasn't been as stable as it used to be. Leeland has already realized that. Now! See that?"

Misaki pointed a finger at the ring, where Leeland had just delivered a vicious-looking kick to Greg's left leg. The man staggered backward, trying to find his balance again. Leeland must have sensed an opening, because he didn't give Greg time to recover. He let himself fall, linked his legs around Greg's ankle, and brought him down. Quick as lightning, Leeland was back on his feet, waiting for Greg to get up.

Jonathan felt his chest swell with pride, accompanied by something else—worry. Leeland was good, no doubt, but Greg was a lot bigger than him and apparently knew what he was doing.

"Seems a bit unfair to me. What if Leeland gets an opponent who doesn't have such a weakness?"

Misaki just shook his head. "That's what the weight classes are for. In the UFC, Leeland would never go against a man like Greg. They would be in different classes. It's hardly fair to send someone with Leeland's build against somebody who looks like Greg or you. That wouldn't make for an interesting fight. I still haven't decided if Leeland is going to fight in the bantamweight or featherweight class, though." Misaki kept his gaze trained on the ring, where Leeland had managed once more to put Greg down.

"Enough!" Misaki stepped forward. Greg and Leeland bowed to each other, then climbed out of the ring. Jonathan followed Misaki to a bench where Greg and Leeland sat down. Both men were covered in sweat and panting.

"That was good, Lee-kun. Better than I expected."

Jonathan felt his hackles rise at the dismissive tone, but he knew Misaki was actually complimenting Leeland, which was why he kept his mouth shut. Leeland didn't seem to take offense. Perhaps he was simply too busy getting his breath back.

Misaki went on. "How much do you weigh at the moment?"

"About a hundred and twenty-five pounds, Ojisan."

Misaki pinched his nose before turning to Greg. "What do you think?"

The bigger man took a sip from a water bottle. "I think featherweight. He's going to build up more muscle during training, and it's always easier to increase weight than to reduce it. Besides, the field is pretty even in both classes, so there's no reason to force him into the bantamweight, and the people from Smash! don't care either way as long as they get their PR."

Misaki nodded. "I agree with you, Greg." He turned to Leeland. "That's it for today, Lee-kun. Greg and I will talk about your training plan, and I'll send it to you later today. I'm sure you know there will be food restrictions as well, so you might want to enjoy a nice dinner tonight, because starting tomorrow you're officially in competition mode. Once I have a date for your first fight, we'll meet with Samantha Jones to go over the PR side of things. She'll probably want to take some promo pictures as well."

Leeland nodded. Jonathan watched his boy very closely, because he didn't behave like his normal self. Usually Leeland was relaxed and happy, but now he seemed stiff and oddly formal. Jonathan could only guess the reason for it. Most probably, it was because the gym was an environment where a certain behavior was expected from Leeland, like when they were at Whisper. Jonathan was vaguely aware that martial arts came with a set of formal behaviors, like bowing to your opponent before a fight started, and using certain expressions to show respect to the other fighter. Being under the scrutiny of his godfather and former trainer could make Leeland feel stressed, Jonathan assumed, especially since he had agreed to work with Misaki again. While Jonathan was still wondering about the dynamics between Leeland and his uncle, Leeland rose from the bench.

"I'll have a quick shower, and then we can go."

Jonathan pressed a kiss on Leeland's forehead. "It's okay, honey. Take your time."

Leeland vanished in the direction of the showers, and Misaki told Jonathan goodbye, saying he had some planning to do. Which left Jonathan alone with Greg, who seemed uncomfortable, judging from the way he was squirming on the bench. Jonathan firmly believed in a direct approach when confronted with problems. It had worked for him ever since he found the courage to be out and proud and embrace his "dark desires," as his deeply religious mother had called his need to dominate his partners. Funnily enough, she'd had no problem with him being gay, just with the fact that he also liked BDSM.

He couldn't tell what Greg's problem was, but since the man was going to work closely with Leeland for the next eleven months, he thought it was a good idea to clear any misunderstanding that might be there.

"Is there something you wanted to say?"

Jonathan watched as Greg averted his eyes, clearly embarrassed.

"No. Yes. I mean… there is something, but it's probably rude…." He trailed off.

Jonathan looked intently at the man, saw nothing explicitly malicious, and decided to cut him some slack.

"Is it about Leeland and me being gay?"

Greg's eyes widened in shock. "No, man, absolutely not! I'm bi, so no problem there."

That caught Jonathan's interest. Greg hadn't pinged his gaydar at all. If the gay thing wasn't the issue, what then? Jonathan watched as Greg fidgeted some more, and finally a light went off in his head. Hopefully this wasn't his mother all over again.

"This is about the BDSM, isn't it? You know we're in the lifestyle?"

Despite Greg's dark skin color, he managed a formidable blush.

"Y-yes. Misaki mentioned it."

"What do you want to know?"

Jonathan saw Greg's shoulders slump. "To be honest, I have no clue. I don't even know why the topic makes me so—jumpy. When Misaki told me about this part of Leeland's life—which is absolutely confidential, I assure you—I found myself fascinated. And seeing you two today, well, I don't know what to think."

Jonathan sighed. He should have expected this. Leeland was close enough to his parents for them to pick up on what he preferred in bed, and via them, Misaki had found out as well. As far as Jonathan knew, Leeland never went into great detail, but his parents knew where he earned his money and how he liked his men. Which was one of the reasons why Leeland was so well versed in self-defense and so incredibly careful when it came to playing with a Dom. His parents had seen to it that he never neglected his safety. When Leeland had told them he was going steady with Jonathan and later that he would move in with him, they had voiced their approval. And of course Jonathan would never forget the open threats he had received from both Layla and Routa Drake at his first meeting with them. They loved their son fiercely, something Jonathan could relate to and respect.

Jonathan wasn't angry at Misaki for telling Greg about this aspect of their relationship. As one of his trainers, Greg would have realized sooner rather than later that something about them was different. And since he knew, he could help keep this special piece of information a secret, though Jonathan still hoped his relationship with his boy would stay under the radar for the duration of Leeland's involvement with the UFC.

Jonathan looked up and saw Greg still watching him with a mixture of embarrassment and curiosity in his eyes. He thought he knew what the man was wondering about. Explaining it was never easy, though, since his and Leeland's relationship was different, even by BDSM standards.

"I guess you have a lot of—set ideas?"

Jonathan tried to phrase his question as vaguely as possible.

Greg nodded wildly. "Yes! I did some research on the web and, well, I'm aware there's lots of stereotyping going on, and don't even get me started on the porn, but still, you and Leeland…." He fell silent again, seemingly not knowing how to express his feelings. Luckily for him, Jonathan had been in the lifestyle long enough to guess where the problem lay.

"You think Leeland should be a lot meeker, don't you? He shouldn't be fighting men like yourself, but walk behind me with his eyes on the ground, waiting to obey my every command. Does that come close?"

"Yes." Greg avoided Jonathan's gaze.

"As you may have already guessed, ours is not a typical BDSM relationship. I like my man to be independent and strong. In my opinion, that makes his submission all the sweeter. I'm not going to lie to you, there are others out there who'd think Leeland is a terrible sub and I'm a useless Dom for how I let him run wild. Relationships in BDSM come in as many shapes as they do in the vanilla world. Leeland and I prefer to meet on equal ground. I love his ability to defend himself, and the fact that a man who could toss me on my ass allows me to dominate him turns me on more than I can say."

Jonathan usually didn't share so much information about himself or his relationship, but he sensed how important it was for Greg to understand the dynamic between him and Leeland. Since Greg and Leeland would be spending a lot of time together and Leeland needed to trust Greg, it was vital to clear any possible misunderstandings.

Greg threw him a sheepish glance. "This whole situation is totally messed-up, with Tony breaking his leg now of all times. It was a low blow, after all the hard training we invested. I have to admit, I thought we would lose Smash! And then Misaki decided to ask Leeland. I can understand why. His name has a good ring in the world of martial arts, even after all those years, and after the match just now, I'm even optimistic that he can win some of his fights." Greg rubbed his left hand over his buzz cut. "What I'm trying to say is, Leeland is our last hope, and somehow I find it difficult to harmonize all the things I know about him."

Jonathan saw an almost pleading look in Greg's face and couldn't help but smile. "You mean all the contradictions."

Greg nodded vehemently.

"It's what makes him so damn interesting. His strength, his skills, his need to be dominated, his ability to kick ass. Leeland is a study in contrasts and sometimes hard to understand. You'll get used to it."

Greg sighed. "I'll do my best. We're going to spend a lot of time together, and I can guarantee he's going to curse my name on a regular basis. I'd prefer if it was solely because of my strict training methods."

Jonathan opened his mouth to answer but was cut off by Leeland, who had apparently finished his shower and returned to them.

"Don't worry about that, Greg. I'm very good at putting the blame where it belongs—at my ojisan's feet. Of course I'm going to wish you into the deepest pits of hell, but we both know the louder I curse, the better you're doing your job."

Leeland was now standing next to Jonathan, his freshly washed and still damp hair in a messy bun at the back of his head. Jonathan put his arm around Leeland's shoulders and kissed him fondly.

"Do you need anything else, honey?"

Leeland shook his head. "I'm ready to leave. You heard my ojisan—we should have a nice meal tonight since it's going to be chicken breast, fish, and steamed vegetables from tomorrow on, with a few cups of brown rice thrown into the mix."

Jonathan detected the tiniest pout in Leeland's voice.

"It'll be fine, honey. Where do you want to go?"

"I haven't decided yet. Can we talk about it on the drive home?"

"As you wish." Jonathan held his hand out to Greg. "It was nice meeting you, Greg. I guess we'll be seeing more of each other in the coming months."

Greg shook his hand. "Likewise, Jonathan. And I'm looking forward to it." He hesitated for a moment. "Thank you for being so open."

"You're welcome."

Jonathan took Leeland's hand and led him out of the gym. While they put on their helmets, Leeland threw Jonathan a questioning glance.

"What was that about?"

Jonathan swung his leg across the saddle of his black Harley.

"Greg seems to be a bit overwhelmed by the whole situation, and he was confused about our relationship. I think I managed to ease some of his worries." He turned around slightly to pat the pillion seat. "Hop on up. Shall we drive home, or do you want to have some coffee first?"

Leeland took his seat with a graceful motion. "No coffee, but could you stop at a pharmacy? I need Epsom salt, arnica cream and oil, and ice packs. In bulk."

"Are you hurt?" Jonathan felt worry creep into his voice. He hadn't seen Leeland taking any direct hits from Greg—he could have missed them, though—but that didn't mean Leeland wasn't hurting.

"It's fine. Greg got me once or twice. For a man his size, he's amazingly fast. But starting tomorrow, I'm going to need those things on a daily basis, and believe me, only few things are worse than crawling home after a strenuous workout only to find your stash of Epsom depleted."

Jonathan blew a quick air kiss on Leeland's nose, the only place despite his eyes he could still see now that they both had their helmets on. "I'd go and buy it for you any time of the day, honey."

"I know. Which is why I love you so much. Nevertheless, I want to be prepared."

"The pharmacy it is."

Jonathan started the Harley and felt the familiar thrill at having Leeland's arms wrap around him.

AFTER THEIR visit to the pharmacy, Jonathan drove them home, where he took a shower while Leeland tried to decide where he wanted to go for his "last meal worth mentioning," as he gloomily put it. Jonathan couldn't imagine things would become so bad, but since he didn't know much about the intricacies of an athlete's diet, he kept his mouth shut. When he came back from the shower, Leeland informed him that they would go to Mamma's. Somehow Jonathan had anticipated this. The restaurant was one of their favorites. After dinner they planned to make a trip to Whisper to see if either Richard or Martin were there and tell them about Leeland's new situation. How they would handle Leeland's responsibilities at the club had yet to be decided. His boy felt reluctant to resign his duties as the middleman between the subs and Doms at Whisper, and Jonathan could understand that. Leeland loved to help, which made him very popular among the subs, some of who were reluctant about turning to Richard and Martin with their everyday troubles.

AFTER A sumptuous dinner where Leeland first ate his weight in pasta and then asked for second helpings of panna cotta and tiramisu, they drove to Whisper. Richard and Martin were both there, together with Dean and Collin.

Jonathan could feel Leeland getting tense when they approached the owners of Whisper at the bar. He knew how much his boy dreaded telling the two Doms about his decision, and now two of his closest friends would be there as well, and nobody knew how any of them would react. Jonathan slung his arm around Leeland, whispering soothing words into his ear.

"Everything will be fine, honey. Just wait and see. These are your friends, your extended family. And I'm here as well. You're not alone in this."

Leeland met Jonathan's gaze. "Thank you." He sounded so grateful, Jonathan just had to squeeze him hard.

After a quick greeting, Jonathan explained that Leeland needed to talk to Richard and Martin, and Richard promptly led them all into his office once he had verified that it was okay for Leeland that Dean and Collin were present. They rearranged the chairs in front of the leather sofa so they all could sit down. Once everybody was seated, Richard looked at Leeland expectantly.

"What is it you want to tell us, Leeland?"

Jonathan felt Leeland taking a deep breath next to him before he started to speak.

"My uncle, Misaki, owns a MMA gym and runs a charity that teaches kids from the street martial arts. He has found a sponsor who was willing to fund the charity if my uncle trained a fighter for them who would participate in the UFC. Three days ago, the fighter was in a car accident and broke his leg. My uncle has asked me to replace him for the next eleven months—and I agreed."

For a moment silence ruled. Richard and Martin's expressions didn't change, but the same couldn't be said for Dean and Collin. Jonathan saw confusion, joy, skepticism, and curiosity in their faces. It was Dean who spoke first.

"Leeland! Judging from the expression on your face, I'm not sure if this is great news or not, but know that I'll be supporting you in whatever way I can. Just tell me what you need. I'll be there for you."

Jonathan saw Leeland gulping. His boy was wound so tight, the simple show of support had him almost in tears. And Collin jumped right in.

"Fighting sounds dangerous, I'm always afraid when Martin or Olivia have to go on assignments where there could be fighting, and you're doing it voluntarily, and I don't know much, but you're a strong man, and I think you can beat them all, and if Martin allows it, I will come to all your fights and cheer you on and help you with the training, though I don't know much about training, but perhaps I can learn, and you can always tell me what you need."

Leeland choked back a sob, and in an instant the three subs were on their feet embracing each other, Dean and Collin whispering their love and support in Leeland's ears. Jonathan was happy his precious lover had such wonderful friends. Some of the tension he had sensed in Leeland ever since they left the gym this afternoon seemed to bleed out of him. He met the gazes of Richard and Martin, and they both nodded, conveying with that simple gesture what their lovers had expressed with a slew of words.

It was Richard who finally ended the cuddling session by clearing his throat. The three subs let go of each other and sat down on the laps of their respective Doms. When he felt Leeland's familiar weight on his thighs, Jonathan exhaled.

Richard looked at Leeland. "Of course you have our full support, Leeland. Whatever you need, you just have to name it." He paused. "I assume this will affect your working schedule?"

Leeland nodded. "I need to train a lot to get in shape. I have a leave of absence from college, and I won't be able to work my regular shifts."

"That won't be a problem. We will keep your position open for when you return." Martin smiled reassuringly. Then he furrowed his brows. "Which reminds me, what about your official function as go-between?"

"That's what I wanted to discuss with you. I don't want to abandon that post, but I can't say yet how often I'll be able to come to the club. I know I'm putting you on the spot with this request, and I'd understand if you'd rather somebody else took over."

The way Leeland's shoulders slumped told Jonathan louder than words how much the idea upset him. He looked at Richard and Martin, who shared a glance. It was Richard who answered.

"Well, it's not ideal, but I think for the time being we can work around the issue until you have found a routine. All the subs have your number, and we just have to stress that they shouldn't be shy about calling you."

"We're here as well," Dean chimed in. "Collin, Curtis, and I are going to spread the word and also tell them they can come to us as well. That should work, shouldn't it?"

He looked up at Richard, who patted him with a loving look in his eyes. Only a year ago, that same look would have driven Jonathan insane because of its sugary-sweetness. Now he knew he was looking into a mirror, for he and Leeland looked at each other the same way, as Peyton had informed him once while making gagging sounds to stress how disgusting he found this display of emotion.

"Yes, darling. That should work." Richard kissed Dean's nose, full of love.

"So that's settled," Martin stated. "Now tell me, Leeland, do you need a sparring partner? I'd love to try my skills against you."

"I'll definitely need sparring partners, Martin. I have to talk to my ojisan first, but you'd be my first choice. Sorry, Master." Leeland threw him an apologetic glance.

Jonathan smiled. "No problem, boy. I know I'm no match for you. And as we have seen today, you need strong opponents. Martin is a better candidate than me." Since Martin owned a security firm, he better had be.

They talked a little longer, Dean and Collin asking Leeland all kinds of questions about how his training and the fights were going to be. Jonathan saw Richard and Martin listening intently to Leeland's explanations of the sometimes complicated proceedings in the UFC and was glad how well they seemed to take the news. He finally pried Leeland from his friends' grasp to take him home. Tonight he wasn't in the mood for a scene. Tonight he wanted to hold his boy, his lover, close and bask in the joy of having found his perfect match.

CHAPTER 9

LEELAND STARED at the plain chicken breast on the kitchen counter with utter contempt. After four weeks, he was wondering how long he would be able to endure this culinary torture before something inside him snapped. The first signs were already there. Last night he'd dreamed about swimming in chocolate mousse, and only Jonathan's resolve had kept him from driving to the next gas station at one in the morning to buy whatever form of sugar was available. The merciless training he could cope with; it was something he remembered from his active days during high school, where it had taken up most of his free time, though he didn't remember it hurting quite so much. He was either getting old or Misaki was pushing him extra hard. It was probably a mixture of both.

Even though his ojisan and the people from Smash! kept telling him it was fine if he didn't win a single match, he was acutely aware of how much they wanted to see him win. Two weeks ago he'd met Samantha Jones—not the one from *Sex and the City*, though she surely could have worked as her double—to take his official publicity shots and talk about how he would represent the brand, a drink he couldn't have because it was anything but a suitable beverage for an athlete. And even if he would have been allowed to drink it, Leeland wouldn't have. One whiff of the concoction that smelled like liquid gummy bears, and he'd known why it had to be aggressively advertised. Nobody in their right mind would voluntarily drink something so obnoxious.

His ojisan had sent Samantha a picture of Leeland beforehand, and she must have liked what she'd seen, because when he arrived at the photographer's studio he was met by three stylists. What should have been a quick shoot in his fighting gear turned into a ten-hour marathon session where he had to dress in everything from a smart business suit by Hugo Boss to a casual jeans and T-shirt outfit by Tommy Hilfiger. It had taken Leeland almost an hour to get rid of all the makeup on his face, though he had to admit, the pictures were stunning. The photographer was a pro who had managed to capture his androgynous nature perfectly. And Leeland understood why Samantha, who was a shining example of an extremely successful American PR lady, wanted those pictures. Her company was already at a disadvantage with the intended athlete being out of the picture. Even though Leeland did have some successes in the world of martial arts under his belt, those had happened too long ago and carried little weight in the UFC. Of course, they were highlighted in the biography Samantha had set up on his new social media account and website, but she needed something substantial to gain interest, and his looks would definitely do the trick.

Leeland didn't think he was being immodest by thinking so. He had a healthy view of himself and knew there were lots of people in the country who loved his type. As Samantha had explained to him quite bluntly, at the moment the only thing he had going for him was his looks. The silent message rang loud and clear. They wanted to see him win, no matter what they said aloud. Fortunately Leeland wanted to win as well. He just didn't have it in him to take part in a competition and not give his best—he had inherited that competitive streak from both his parents, as well as the need to fulfill the duties he took on.

Again Leeland focused on the chicken breast, wondering how he could manage to get some taste on it. So far Jonathan hadn't complained openly about the extremely healthy and boring food Leeland served him, but the Dom loved his burgers and fries and other greasy delights. He'd better stop thinking about all the good things he was missing out on, or he would probably throw the chicken breast in the trash—which the poor animal that had died for him didn't deserve. Perhaps if he marinated it in garlic oil… no, that would take too long. He was hungry now.

The front door clicked, and Leeland heard Jonathan's heavy steps in the hall. He smiled and turned around, waiting for his lover to enter the kitchen. There was a crash, followed by some colorful curses when Jonathan apparently found the stack of wooden planks Mike and Frank had left in the hall. Peyton was almost done with the renovation, and even Jonathan had admitted the apartment looked great now. Apart from the walls that had to go, the flooring and the ceilings had been changed as well, but the outcome of this complete makeover was breathtaking. They now had oiled, sand-colored hardwood floors in every room except the kitchen and bathroom, which were tiled with black marble. The ceilings were white to highlight the different color schemes Peyton had chosen for the individual rooms. It was all light and modern, with lots of steel, glass, and wood, and the occasional splash of color in a cloth, painting, or furniture to draw the eye. Even Collin's carpet had found its place in the guestroom as a wall decoration. All in all, Leeland loved the new look of Jonathan's—and his—place.

"Hey, Leeland, what are you brooding about?" Jonathan's voice right next to his ear startled Leeland from his musings. He turned to kiss his handsome Dom before answering.

"Hello, Jonathan. About how nice the apartment looks." He glanced at the chicken breast. "And how bleak dinner is going to be."

Jonathan laughed and pulled him into a hug. "It's for a good cause and only temporary. We can do this."

"You really don't have to join me in this nutritional madness."

"I know, honey. And I do get some bad, bad food now and then, when you're not there to witness my fall from grace and be tempted by it, but I want to show you my full support. Besides, Garrett has mentioned how my new diet affects my performance in the gym and my body positively."

Leeland pictured Garrett Kiernan, Dom at Whisper, Emilio's boyfriend, and gym owner. He looked up at Jonathan and raised a brow in question.

Jonathan huffed. "Fine, he said it's a good thing I stopped stuffing my face like a pig that's being fattened for Christmas. And if I kept with his new training routine, I would perhaps manage to lose all the fat clogging my arteries and padding my muscles and look halfway decent."

Leeland nodded. That sounded a lot more like Master Garrett. The man was a fitness enthusiast and as blunt as a baseball bat to the head, especially when it came to people he knew well and liked. Somehow Leeland was glad that Greg was in charge of his training. Master Garrett would have been a lot worse.

"You're not fat." Leeland meant it. Jonathan was built like the men who participated in the Highland Games, where competitors had to throw tree trunks and lift heavy barrels. Stocky, compact, the sheer power of his muscles hidden underneath some padding that Leeland loved, especially when they were cuddling.

"You're biased."

"I'm the only one whose opinion counts."

Jonathan laughed. "I'll tell that to Garrett next time he harasses me. Now, what are we going to do with this chicken breast?"

"Wrap it in bacon, dump it in gravy with extra cream, and top it with cheese."

"Sounds delicious, honey. Problem is we have none of these ingredients here. There is salad, though." Jonathan sounded almost apologetic.

Leeland whined. "I hate this! Have I mentioned how much I hate this?"

Jonathan kissed him. "You have, and I know. It's fine, you're entitled to hate it. You just can't have anything else for the time being. But I promise you, when this is over, I'll take you to Mamma's, and then you can eat until you explode."

Leeland groaned. The things Jonathan said to him! The promise made his cock harden in his pants—or at least his cock made an *effort* to harden. Training had just been too tough today.

Jonathan kissed him on the cheek before he took a look in the fridge. "Let's see what we have. Parmesan, salad, tomatoes, and olives. How about we fry the chicken breast with some of the chili oil I bought last week and mix it with the vegetables. The cheese should add some flavor. Did you eat your almonds already? If not, we can chop them and add them for crunchiness."

Leeland thought about the proposal. It sounded decent. Not like pasta and steak and tiramisu, but edible. And he didn't have a choice anyway.

"No, I haven't had my five almonds yet. Crunchy salad with chicken breast it is."

Jonathan chuckled and pressed a kiss to Leeland's head before he put on his apron that had the body of a Leather Daddy printed on it. "If you're a good boy, I'll add some extra coconut water to your protein shake tomorrow."

Leeland didn't dignify that with an answer. Instead, he simply slapped Jonathan with one of the dish towels. Coconut water didn't even make it on his list of food he liked. Unfortunately, he had to drink it every day. Mixed up with protein powder, oatmeal, and frozen berries, it wasn't too bad, but Leeland resented it enough to think he could taste it everywhere. With a sigh, he watched as Jonathan started frying the chicken breast.

"Have you drunk enough water?"

There was a hint of worry in Jonathan's voice that made Leeland's heart beat faster. When Leeland's training started, Jonathan had sat down with Greg to find out what he could do to help. Making sure Leeland was always sufficiently hydrated was one of those things. When Jonathan had realized how much Leeland resented drinking bland water, he had started experimenting until he found a way to make the liquid more attractive for Leeland. He could now choose from four different flavors, all approved by his ojisan, and Leeland was more than grateful that Jonathan had made the effort. His favorite was water mixed with half a cup of peppermint tea and a squeezed lemon.

"Yes. Even more than required." Leeland smiled when he saw Jonathan's pleased grin.

"I think the chicken is good now." Jonathan turned the stove off and dumped the bits of chicken breast on top of the salad Leeland had prepared while Jonathan cooked.

"There, doesn't look too bad, does it?"

Leeland stared at the salad. "No, it doesn't. I still wish it were something else."

Jonathan patted his back. "Tomorrow you get your wish. Then it's going to be tilapia."

Leeland groaned, remembering it was fish day the following day. At least it would be a different flavor. He took the bowl with the salad, carried it to the small kitchen table, and started putting the food on the two plates Jonathan set down. They ate in comfortable silence, and Leeland had to admit it wasn't that bad. In Jonathan's company, almost nothing was truly unbearable.

AFTER DINNER they were just done washing the dishes when Jonathan's cell pinged. He took it off the kitchen counter where he always placed it during their meals and looked at it. For a moment his face lit up, only to turn into a disappointed expression.

"What is it?" Leeland was curious.

"Nothing."

Leeland kept on looking at Jonathan with an intent expression. He always knew when his lover was trying to be evasive.

Jonathan shrugged. "Just a reminder for the demonstration tonight. You know, Don and Thomas are showing the use of sounds at Whisper."

Of course Leeland remembered. He and Jonathan had been looking forward to that date ever since the fall schedule of events had come out. Richard believed firmly in regular demonstrations at Whisper, and Don was one of the best Doms in the scene. When he and Thomas took the stage, it was always a treat. Sounding was also something neither Jonathan nor Leeland had ever tried before. After some discussion they had decided they were interested but wouldn't do anything without proper instructions first, since the technique was not without risks.

Leeland's shoulders slumped. Just thinking about putting on some leather and going out tonight made his sore muscles protest loudly. "I'm so sorry, Jonathan. I completely forgot. And I'm just too tired. With my first fight scheduled in two weeks, Greg and Ojisan are working me extra hard."

Which was an understatement. The two acted like slave drivers. He saw Jonathan shrug.

"It's fine, honey. We'll go some other time. This is surely not the last demonstration on sounds Don will give. And if it is, we'll just ask him for a private lesson."

Leeland shook his head. "No, I think you should go, Jonathan. Just because I've turned into a ninety-year-old who has to go to bed at nine, you don't have to skip all the fun. You're already doing so much, and I'd hate for you to miss this. At least one of us should enjoy himself tonight."

Jonathan seemed torn. His amazing dark eyes looked down on Leeland, obviously trying to gauge how serious he was.

Leeland slung his arms around Jonathan's neck and pulled him down for a kiss. "I mean it. I'm boring company and will go to bed soon. Go out and have some fun. I expect you to come back an expert on sounding."

After another minute of contemplating, Jonathan nodded. "Fine. I'll go." He kissed Leeland on the nose. "I'd better take a shower now."

While Jonathan showered, Leeland finished cleaning the kitchen. When his Dom appeared in his tight leather trousers and a black silk shirt, Leeland felt a stab of something he couldn't—and didn't want to—name in his chest. All this gorgeousness wasn't for him tonight. Jonathan kissed him goodbye, the smell and feel of the butter-soft leather and fine silk under Leeland's hands almost more than he could endure. Now his cock was definitely interested, but Jonathan was already on his way out of the door.

When he heard the front door close, Leeland felt the same stab in his chest again. This time he recognized what it was, though. A mixture of anger and self-pity. Anger because Jonathan had taken his offer to leave, and self-pity because now he was all alone in the apartment with only his aching muscles and a semi-hard-on as company. Leeland felt tears pooling in his eyes. He knew his emotional reaction stemmed from physical exhaustion and the pressure he felt weighing on his shoulders, which didn't make it better or easier to bear. Rational thought could only carry him so far until it lost its power. What he needed now was chocolate. Or ice cream. Even better, both. He could always shovel the ice cream with a bar of dark chocolate. A quick inspection of the freezer reminded him of that ugly first day of training when he and Jonathan had gone through their food and thrown out everything he wasn't allowed to eat. Damn, he needed the container of Häagen Dazs Cookies and Cream they had given to Jonathan's mechanics. Who did such a stupid thing as giving away frozen sugar? Leeland knew looking in the drawer where he usually stashed his sweets would just make him depressed. He sank down on one of the chairs at the kitchen table and tried very hard not to start sobbing uncontrollably. He was *not* going to cry over sugar denied.

Or a boyfriend who went to a sounding demonstration without him. He could do this, he was stronger than his urges, he was a fucking UFC fighter, a hard, tough man, a warrior, he was....

Leeland felt his tears starting to fall. This was one of the things he hadn't missed about competing—the emotional roller coaster induced by exhaustion and terrible food. He was so caught up in his misery, he almost didn't hear the front door opening. Quickly Leeland wiped the tears from his face and tried to get the sobbing under control.

"Did you forget something?" he yelled with only a soft quiver to his voice.

Jonathan's heavy steps resounded once again in the hall. There was no crash this time, so he must have remembered the planks. When he entered the kitchen, looking like Leeland's personal god of BDSM with his black leather jacket still on, he took one glance at Leeland, opened his arms, and Leeland didn't hesitate to jump from the chair and run into his embrace. Surrounded by the comforting scent of leather and Jonathan, Leeland barely heard the words his Dom spoke.

"Yes. I forgot how much I love you. I forgot that we wanted to do this together. I forgot how important you are to me. I forgot that being with you is more important to me than attending a demonstration I wouldn't be able to enjoy without you by my side. I'm sorry, Leeland. Sometimes I'm slow."

Leeland laughed and cried at the same time. When he calmed down a bit, he looked up into Jonathan's face. "No, you're not slow. You're the best. I told you to go. It's not your fault when I change my mind or, worse, don't know what I want."

"Oh, boy. You're under extreme pressure at the moment. Don't think I don't know it. I can see it in the way you tense up every time you enter your uncle's gym. I can read it in your eyes when you tell me about your training." Jonathan kissed his forehead, and Leeland could feel the love rolling off his Dom in waves. "One of the reasons I love you so much is because no matter what you do, you always give it your all. I'm just afraid sometimes Misaki and Greg are pushing you too far. You don't have a safeword with them, and even if you had, I don't think you'd use it."

Leeland snuggled back into Jonathan's arms. "You're right, I'm insanely stressed. All that pressure boils down to the fact that I don't want to sacrifice an entire year of my life and have nothing to show for it. Despite not wanting to disappoint my ojisan."

When he spoke the words out loud, Leeland realized how true they were. The food wasn't the problem. Nor was the training or the lack of sugar. The real problem was his fear of failing. And there was nothing he could do about that. At least, not immediately. Once he had his first fight and—hopefully—won it, he would become a little calmer. Or so he hoped.

Jonathan lifted him up and carried him to the couch in the living room. There he sat down, arranged Leeland on his lap until he was facing Jonathan with his legs on either side of Jonathan's thighs, his head pressed against the gap in Jonathan's leather jacket, and started stroking Leeland's back in soothing motions.

"It's fine, honey. Everything is going to be fine. I'm here for you, as are all your friends and your family. And you can't fail in this. Your participation alone is a win. Just remember, this is about your uncle's charity first and about winning second. You can't lose your perspective, Leeland."

Leeland felt a shudder run through his body, and then he started to relax. Something inside him loosened, and for the first time since he started training, the knot of dread in his stomach unclenched.

"I love you so much. Need you like breathing, Jonathan."

Jonathan hugged him even closer.

"And I love you, honey. More than life itself."

CHAPTER 10

LEELAND STOOD in a corner of one of the changing rooms in the T-Mobile Arena in Las Vegas and tried to tune out the distant roars of the hyped-up crowd. The fight going on out there was already in the final, third round, and it wouldn't be long until it was his turn. He was properly warmed up, had received some last-minute briefing from his ojisan and Greg, and felt the tension coiling inside his belly. For his first fight, Sean Shelby and Mick Maynard, the fight matchmakers of the UFC, had paired him with Carlos Scamander, another newbie who would give his debut tonight. Carlos had his home base in Utah, came from boxing, and was everything Leeland was not—at least when it came to looks, which was probably the reason they had been chosen to fight against each other. He and Carlos were a study in contrasts. Where Leeland was slim, lean, and androgynous, Carlos was almost painfully masculine, with a stocky build and bulging muscles. He was a little shorter than Leeland, with a military buzz cut that highlighted his rough facial features, a square jaw, and a flat nose that had obviously been broken more than once—a typical boxer injury. Leeland had seen some videos of Carlos in the boxing ring, and he was suitably impressed. The man was quick on his feet and could let his fists fly like a double-bass drum. This wasn't going to be an easy match.

"Leeland, it's time." Greg poked his head through the door of the changing room. Leeland gave him a curt nod, then checked his four-ounce fighting gloves one last time. The fabric of the black fighting shorts he wore clung to his skin without restricting his movements and also highlighted his tight ass. It was something Leeland could have worn at Whisper, and the thought had him smiling. To imagine the same clothing was appropriate for both a gay BDSM club and one of the most macho-driven sports in the world did show a certain irony. Maybe there was a God, and he or she was laughing their head off every time a UFC fight started. Or maybe the world was just a funny place, and it would be good if more people came to appreciate that.

Greg led him through the long corridor toward the arena. The smell of stale sweat, used socks, freshly spilled beer, and other, more unpleasant scents hung in the air and offended his nostrils. It had been too long since his last official fight, and Leeland found he hadn't missed the stink at all, although here in the T-Mobile Arena, it had a mature quality different from the tamer smell of high school gyms, which reeked more of teenage hormones on the rampage. Yes, the beer definitely made a difference, even though Leeland wasn't sure if it was for better or worse.

When he and Greg reached the entrance that would lead him to his side of the cage, he heard the speaker announce his name.

"And from Miami, Florida, Leeland Drake!"

The crowd erupted in applause, not because people already knew him, but because most of them were already drunk on alcohol and violence. Leeland stepped out into the blinding light of the arena. For a brief moment, he allowed his gaze to flicker toward the first row to his right, where he knew Jonathan, his parents, and his friends from Whisper were seated. Leeland met Jonathan's eyes for a moment, and the love and encouragement he saw there was all he needed. Taking a deep breath, Leeland sank into his warrior headspace, tuning out the sounds of the people, centering on himself, concentrating on his opponent. Carlos Scamander was already in the cage in his corner, staring at him, no doubt trying to assess him like he was evaluating Carlos.

The cage was closed, and it was only Leeland, Carlos, and the referee on the canvas. Leeland noticed some blood on the mat from the previous fights, but it didn't really matter. After this night, the canvas would never be used again. For each fight night, an individual canvas was painted and afterward thrown away. It was a custom in the UFC, one that seemed ridiculous at first glance, but which Leeland understood perfectly. Getting bloodstains out of any fabric was a bitch. It was also a matter of money. The logos of the sponsors were painted on the canvas, and as they changed, so did the fabric on which the fighters competed. A quick glance to the ground while he made his way to the middle of the octagon showed Leeland the logo of Smash! in one of the corners. Samantha Jones would be happy.

He met his opponent in the middle of the cage, and they shook hands. Carlos had a firm grip but didn't try to make it a contest, which earned him a few merits in Leeland's book. He despised nothing more than men who tried to make a point with their strength alone. Then the referee raised his hand and stepped back. The fight was officially on.

Leeland brought his hands up quickly and sidestepped Carlos's attempt at getting him in a surprise attack. The man was even faster than Leeland had anticipated, and he wasted no time going after Leeland with a volley of blows Leeland managed to block, but which he would definitely feel later in his lower arms. Carlos was obviously trying to turn this into a boxing match, which would be to his advantage. Leeland had no intention of allowing that—couldn't allow it if he wanted to have a chance at winning. When Carlos went for a right hook, Leeland ducked under it and landed a firm blow to Carlos's ribs. Carlos retreated in surprise, and Leeland used the moment of distraction to strike twice with his left leg on Carlos's thigh in order to upset his balance. It worked, and Carlos stumbled backward, trying to get out of Leeland's reach before he could get another leg kick in.

To defend himself, Carlos was now forced to use martial art techniques, which gave Leeland an advantage. They traded more blows and jabs, the fight waging between boxing and a mix of karate and tae kwon do. Leeland managed to get Carlos a few times on the head and was sure it had to hurt—just like the punches Carlos rained on him. They were evenly matched, and the whistle marking the end of their first five minutes came as a relief.

Leeland retreated into his corner, where his ojisan was waiting for him with water and a slew of instructions.

"He's quick, so you must be quicker. You must take control of this fight, Leeland. Don't let him revert to boxing so much. He's too strong. Force him to fight with martial arts. Now go!"

Leeland shook his head. One minute wasn't enough to get good tactical advice or recover sufficiently. Nothing his ojisan had told him was news, but he did feel exhausted already. Five minutes could be damn long against a determined opponent, no matter how hard a fighter had trained. There was a huge difference between training in the relative tranquility of a gym and being out in the lion's den of the octagon. At least he didn't yet feel the bruises forming everywhere Carlos had hit him. There was too much adrenaline coursing through his system.

They met in the middle of the cage again, and Leeland thought he could detect a certain wariness in Carlos. He wasn't the only one who felt the strain of the fight.

The referee raised his hand, and their violent dance began anew. Leeland ducked sideways under one of Carlos's straight punches and kneed him in the kidneys. Carlos stumbled forward, regained his balance far more quickly than Leeland had anticipated, and countered with a spinning back fist Leeland couldn't completely evade. The force of the impact had his ears ringing, and it was only his excellent reflexes that saved him from subsequently getting hit by a spinning back kick.

Leeland shook his head to clear his mind. His vision suddenly seemed to become more focused, and his thoughts turned into a sharp, predatory *thing* that had only one goal—winning. Back when he was active, this had happened to him in almost every fight, this transformation into a fighting machine, but it had been so long, Leeland had forgotten the eerie clarity and frightening calmness that came with it. He was no longer thinking about what he did; he simply moved. Blocking, ducking, punching, striking—it all flowed together in perfect harmony. But Carlos was strong, stocky, he could take the blows Leeland dished out. He needed a different tactic.

The second blow of the whistle couldn't pry Leeland from his trance, and his ojisan took one look at his face and knew better than to tell him what to do.

The third round started. Carlos seemed to be getting tired, or desperate, or probably both, just like Leeland. But unlike Leeland, he was acting recklessly in his eagerness to end the fight with a knockout. Reckless opponents made mistakes. Leeland had already realized he wouldn't be able to knock Carlos out, not in the few minutes they had left, and he didn't want to find out who the three judges saw as the winner. It was time to end this.

Carlos came on to him with a wide swing of his left arm. Leeland sidestepped and saw his chance. He let himself fall and swiped Carlos's legs from under him. While Carlos was still falling, Leeland twisted his body. His legs closed around Carlos's upper body and brought him down in the side-control position known from wrestling. Leeland usually avoided going for ground-and-pound since his opponents were normally heavier and stronger than him, which made it difficult for him to control them. But Carlos was in his weight class. He might have a few pounds on Leeland, but not enough to make a difference. All Leeland had to do now was squeeze Carlos's upper body until he submitted or the referee ended the fight.

After what seemed like an eternity, Carlos tapped the canvas once, submitting to Leeland. Leeland breathed a sigh of relief and loosened his hold on Carlos. His thighs were on fire and he wasn't sure how much longer he would have been able to keep the other man under control. They both got up, and when the referee declared Leeland the winner, the shouts of the crowd turned into a roar. Leeland felt a fresh wave of adrenaline surge through his body.

He had won his first fight.

LEELAND LET the scalding water in the small shower of the changing room wash over his body. The adrenaline from the fight and the rush of his victory were slowly starting to fade, and his body took the opportunity to remind him of every blow and punch and hit he hadn't been able to duck. It sucked and wouldn't get better until it had gotten a lot worse. All Leeland wanted was to go back to the hotel, soak in the tub there, preferably with Jonathan, then fall into bed and sleep for a week. Unfortunately he still had some PR to do. Nothing major—he wasn't famous enough for that—but a small press conference with a few bloggers and a journalist from Fox for the fans. While Leeland washed his hair with his favorite shampoo, he started remembering all the things he had tuned out after the fight. The way his family and friends had risen from their seats when he was announced the winner. The pride on his ojisan's face. The satisfied smile on Samantha Jones's lips. The silly little victory dance Peyton did on top of his seat. Leeland grinned. He knew Peyton had bet some money on him, a hundred dollars, to be precise. The odds had not been in favor of Leeland, which meant Peyton was going to collect a hefty sum, and many other people would hopefully reassess their habit of snap judgments. One could always dream.

With a sigh Leeland turned off the shower, slung a towel around his slim hips, and exited the stall. At the locker he had been assigned, he quickly dried himself before getting out his cocoa body butter. After a fight there was nothing better to soothe his nerves. While he massaged the pleasantly warming butter into his skin, enjoying the subtle scent, he suddenly heard somebody clearing their throat at his back. Leeland turned around to see Carlos standing there, he, too, only wearing a towel. Since most of the changing rooms were connected by doors, Leeland assumed Carlos had come from the neighboring room. The man definitely didn't know where to look, if his beet-red face was any indication. Leeland furrowed his brows. Because of his lifestyle, he didn't have a problem with nudity, but he didn't want to make the other man uncomfortable. Since he was already done with the body butter, he snatched his silk boxers out of the locker and put them on, as well as a dark red button-down he was supposed to wear for the press conference. Once he was clothed, Carlos seemed to relax a bit. He looked Leeland in the eye and extended his hand.

"Good fight. Congratulations."

Leeland smiled and took the offered hand. He could tell Carlos was serious.

"Thank you, man. You didn't make it easy for me. You're superfast."

Carlos blushed a bit at the praise. "Not fast enough, apparently."

"Says the man whose blows I'm going to feel for the next week."

Leeland kept his tone light. Even though they had just met and beaten the shit out of each other, he liked Carlos. Carlos opened his mouth to say something but was cut short by an angry voice coming from the connecting door.

"Carlos, stop stroking your opponent's ego by whining like a beaten dog! Get your ass dressed and out of here, pronto!"

Carlos rolled his eyes. "Yes, Mason."

A huff sounded from the door before it was forcefully closed. Carlos shrugged.

"Sorry about that. Mason is my stepdad and kind of—driven. He sees me as this huge talent who's going to be famous and rich and is pissed that I lost my first fight. After he saw your pictures, he couldn't stop bragging about how I would wipe the floor with your sissy ass. He can be kind of an asshole."

Leeland grimaced. "Don't sweat it, I get that a lot. I mean, I have no illusions about my looks. It is what it is. For what it's worth, I enjoyed our fight."

Carlos turned around. "Really? Because I did too. I know I'm not supposed to talk to the enemy, but I don't like all this alpha male bullshit posturing."

Leeland laughed out loud. He started to like Carlos more and more. "Seems like we picked the wrong sport, then." He turned serious again. "How about we exchange phone numbers? We can keep in touch and share our training-induced misery."

Carlos groaned. "Don't remind me. If I have to eat another plain chicken breast, I'm going to scream. And don't even get me started on the almond butter. Whoever thought that was a good thing to add to an athlete's diet must have been a sadist or out of their mind—or both. What I wouldn't give for a pizza with extra cheese."

Leeland put his hand on his mouth in mock consternation. "Are you crazy? The bad carbohydrates! All that grease ruining your muscle definition! What are you thinking?"

Carlos managed to look contrite despite the amused glittering in his eyes. "My apologies. I didn't know I was talking to the food police. Of course there's nothing better than steamed vegetables and plain brown rice. I mean, who wants to have their meals actually *taste* like something?"

"Not me. I abhor everything sugary or with fat. Give me the veggies and the chicken! And who doesn't love a delicious protein shake topped with spinach? The color alone makes my mouth water!"

They both giggled. Leeland took his phone out of the locker, swiped it open, and held it under Carlos's nose. "Your number, please."

With a faint smile, Carlos typed his contact info in. When he got the phone back, Leeland sent his own contact to Carlos's number.

"Let's keep in touch."

Carlos nodded. "I'd love that. I was so nervous about all this, but meeting you, I can see the bright spots."

Leeland bowed. "Thank you. Now for the less pleasant part. I do believe we have a press conference to attend."

Carlos's shoulders faltered. "Don't remind me. I mean, why do they even want to talk to me? I lost!"

Leeland put a hand on Carlos's shoulder. "But next time you might win. Today everybody has seen what a strong fighter you are. See it as groundwork for your career."

Carlos looked directly at Leeland. "Thank you. That actually makes sense."

Leeland snorted. "Put a red circle in your calendar. I rarely make sense."

"To me, you do." Carlos turned in the direction of the connecting door, holding his towel with one hand. "I'll be in touch!"

Leeland watched him go, happy that he had made a new friend. Since Carlos would be interviewed first, he still had some time to blow-dry his hair before it was his turn.

WHEN LEELAND left the locker room, he was immediately crowded by Samantha, who did nothing to hide her glee while she ushered him toward the interview room.

"Leeland, you were great! This is wonderful! I listened around a bit, and people are already taking an interest in you. Nobody expected you to win, so now they're curious."

"I'm glad things are working out for you."

She flashed him one of her quick, professional smiles, all red lipstick and blindingly white teeth and completely devoid of true empathy. "It does. If it goes on like this, it's going to be a breeze."

Leeland didn't comment on that. He was simply too tired to deal with Samantha apart from the few words he'd said. He wanted Jonathan and sleep, but he couldn't have either until later. They had decided that for the time being, they wouldn't broadcast their relationship, which meant Jonathan had already left for the hotel. His ojisan and Greg would escort him back there as soon as the journalists and bloggers were done with him.

They reached another nondescript door behind which the interview would take place. A table with microphones was set on this end of the room, facing several rows of ugly plastic chairs where three bloggers, two male, one female, were sitting. A little to the right, a man in his forties was standing next to a camera with the Fox emblem at the side. Since Fox had bought the exclusive rights for the UFC fights, they had created a channel that solely focused on MMA. Those rights were about to run out by the end of this year and would be open for renegotiation in 2018, but those were things Leeland was only marginally interested in. Leeland sat down in front of the microphones, took a sip from the water bottle somebody had placed there for him, and waited for the questions to begin. The man from Fox went first.

"My name is Graham Carter from Fox. Mr. Drake, how do you feel after this spectacular win?"

Inwardly, Leeland winced at the stupid question as well as the way it was phrased—there was nothing spectacular about his win. Carter was simply fishing for some slights against Carlos. It was a typical interview tactic, one most of the testosterone-driven alpha males in the UFC embraced wholly. Leeland assumed that after a fight it was simply easier to let the hormones do the talking—and a lot more entertaining as well. It just wasn't his style.

Leeland gave the man his most dazzling smile. "To be honest, Mr. Carter, I feel sore. Carlos Scamander throws a mean hook."

Amused, Leeland watched the hint of confusion on Graham Carter's face when he didn't give him a rant about how he'd obliterated his opponent. To his credit, it didn't take long until he overcame his shock.

"Yes, he does indeed, as the videos of the fight show." Carter hesitated a moment. "From your biography, I see this wasn't your first fight, yet today was announced as your debut?"

"I can see how that might be confusing." Leeland knew he sounded condescending, but he couldn't help himself. He was tired and wanted Jonathan. "Today was my first fight in the UFC, so it was a debut. I did compete during high school and a bit afterward, but solely in martial arts. And I think you'll agree with me when I say the UFC is something very different indeed."

Carter nodded. Leeland could see him preparing to ask the next question on his sheet when the female blogger chimed in.

"Hi, Mr. Drake, I'm Leandra Donnell, I write for my blog Male Mysteries Explained. Most of my readers are female and not well versed in the world of MMA, which is the reason I'm here. If you had to explain the UFC to them, what would you say?"

Leeland perked up. An interesting question! He hadn't anticipated that.

"Well, Miss Donnell, if I had to explain the UFC, I'd say it's a perfect place for men to vent their anger and frustration in a safe environment. It's also the place where different ways of fighting— boxing, wrestling, and martial arts—come together in an aesthetic and inspiring way. My fight against Carlos Scamander today is a perfect example. He comes from boxing, I come from martial arts, and in our fight, we combined both styles to create something new. If it weren't for the blood and all the bruises I can feel forming on my body, I'd almost say it's like a dance."

Leandra Donnell gave him an almost flirtatious smile, obviously satisfied with his answer. "So you don't see Carlos Scamander as an opponent?"

"Oh, I do. That's what the UFC is all about. But I also see him as a partner, as somebody I can learn a great deal from. The appeal of MMA is that the fighters get a chance to explore and expand their skills. In every fight we have to come up with new moves, as do our opponents. That way it's never boring."

"Beautifully put, Mr. Drake. Thank you very much."

Leeland smiled at her before he turned his attention back to Carter, who fired his next standard question.

After another twenty minutes, Leeland was finally allowed to leave. His ojisan called a taxi, and together with Greg, they went back to their hotel.

CHAPTER 11

JONATHAN STARTED to smile when he heard the soft click of the door to his and Leeland's hotel room opening. His boy was finally here! Jonathan went to greet him, his arms opening the minute he saw Leeland's tired expression. Even though Leeland rarely complained openly, Jonathan knew he was having a hard time, putting himself under more pressure than was—at least in Jonathan's opinion—strictly necessary.

When Leeland flew into his arms—Jonathan would never dare to call the heavy shuffle of Leeland's feet anything else—he picked him up immediately and carried him into the huge bedroom, where he placed his boy gently on the bed. Leeland didn't protest when Jonathan took off his clothes, lifted him up again, and carried him into the connected bathroom, where he had already prepared a tub full of hot water and Epsom salt. Jonathan checked the temperature and opened the faucet to add some more hot water before gently sliding Leeland into the tub. He then stripped off his own clothes to follow his boy. Once they were both comfortably seated, Leeland draped against his massive chest like a puppet with its strings cut, Jonathan started tracing all the places where his boy had been hit in today's fight. He remembered each blow as if he had received it himself, and his heart ached when he thought of the fights to come. Leeland moaned low in his throat, relaxing under the soft touch just like Jonathan wanted him to.

Watching Leeland in a serious match had both been harder and easier than Jonathan had imagined. Harder because he could barely stand seeing his precious honey being hurt—and not in the good way—and easier because he found he trusted Leeland's skills more than he had realized. It was also heady, hearing all the praise for his boy from the mouths of strangers. More than once Jonathan had thought his chest would explode from swelling up in utter pride. Luckily their friends from Whisper had helped to keep him grounded, especially

Richard and Curtis. Martin had had his hands full with Collin. The slightly scattered artist hadn't taken well to seeing his friend getting hurt but had refused to leave the arena before the fight was over. Jonathan wondered briefly what it would take to calm Collin down and was glad it wasn't his problem. As much as he adored Collin, the artist definitely wasn't the kind of partner Jonathan needed.

Which brought him back to the softly snoring boy in his arms. The water was still warm enough to warrant staying in the tub for a little longer. Jonathan loathed having to wake Leeland after the stressful day he'd had. When the water finally started cooling, Jonathan reluctantly shook Leeland. Once they were out of the tub, he quickly toweled them both off before he carried Leeland back to the bed.

"Do you want a massage, or would you rather sleep?"

Leeland made a moaning sound in the back of his throat. "Both."

Jonathan chuckled. "Okay, honey. Let me get the oil."

He hurried to retrieve the grape-seed oil from their luggage. On his way back to the bed, he unscrewed the lid, promptly spilling some of the oil onto the carpet.

"Damn!"

Leeland turned his head lazily. "What?"

Jonathan chuckled. "I was too eager, honey. Now I have to give the carpet a massage."

"No way!" Leeland pouted and almost convinced Jonathan that he was serious. "You can't have an affair with that carpet. I mean, look at it, all boring brown and beige colors. That's not for you."

"I'm not having an affair, honey. I just have to give it a massage so the oil doesn't go to waste. It was too expensive."

Leeland's left brow went up. "It's not like you can't afford it."

Grinning, Jonathan pretended to kneel down. Leeland whined. The shock of possibly being denied his massage seemed to have revived his spirits.

"Jonathan! Get your ass up here! Now!"

"Aren't we bossy today? Well, I guess you earned it. Sorry, Mr. Carpet, I'm afraid I have to cut our liaison short. My boyfriend awaits."

Leeland just huffed indignantly, and Jonathan had to suppress a snicker. It was good to see Leeland relaxing, not only physically but mentally as well. The mattress dipped under Jonathan's weight as he kneeled between Leeland's spread thighs. He trickled a generous amount of oil into the cup of his left hand before letting it fall slowly on Leeland's back. His boy's ecstatic moan had his cock hardening in ten seconds flat. *Down, boy!* Jonathan scolded himself. Leeland was in no condition to have sex at the moment. The mere memory of some of the punches Carlos Scamander had landed on Leeland made Jonathan flinch. It amazed him what his boy was able to endure.

With sure, practiced movements, Jonathan started working on Leeland's stiff muscles, eliciting a groan here and there when he found an especially tender spot. After about ten minutes, Leeland was snoring softly again. With a fond smile, Jonathan finished the massage, turned his precious boy around until he was spooning him, pulled the covers up over both of them, and reached for the light switch. It was time to get some sleep.

They slept in until ten the next morning. Since the private plane Richard had chartered for all of them would depart at twelve, they ordered room service and used the time until their breakfast arrived to pack. Leeland was moving carefully, wincing softly now and then. Jonathan took him in his arms.

"Honey, why don't you sit down and let me take care of our luggage? I'm a big boy. I can handle it." He waggled his brows for emphasis.

Leeland laughed and pressed a quick kiss to his lips. "Thank you, Jonathan. I do feel a bit—sore." He made a face. "I've forgotten how crappy you feel after a fight."

Jonathan narrowed his gaze on Leeland. "You'll tell me if something is wrong, won't you?"

Leeland's expression turned serious. "Of course, Master. I may be competitive, but I'm not stupid. Besides, I like it when you pamper me." The last was clearly said to lighten the mood, but Jonathan knew everything he needed to know—Leeland's use of the word "master" said it all. His boy would bring his troubles to Jonathan like he always did. Jonathan encircled Leeland in his muscular arms, breathing in the comforting scent of his boy.

"Thank you, Leeland. You can always count on me. Always."

Leeland shuddered in his arms. "I love you, Master."

"And I love you, boy."

AFTER THEY had eaten their breakfast, they met Leeland's parents, Misaki, Greg, Richard, Dean, Martin, Collin, Curtis, Peyton, and Emilio in the lobby. While their friends and family congratulated Leeland, Jonathan went to the reception desk to check out. Richard had already called three minivans to drive them to the private hangar where their plane would take off. At Martin's request, he and Collin drove with Jonathan and Leeland. It took Jonathan only one look at Collin to know the reason. Collin was plastered against Martin's side, his eyes huge with worry and guilt. The worry Jonathan could understand; the guilt remained a mystery.

When they entered their transport, Leeland saw to it that Collin was sitting next to him. As soon as the vehicle started to roll, Leeland turned to Collin.

"Everything all right, Collin?"

Jonathan felt his heart swell in his chest. His boy was so gentle, so considerate, sensing Collin's distress and trying everything in his power to soothe it. Was there a Dom in history who ever had a more perfect partner?

Collin took a trembling breath, his lower lip quivering dangerously.

"I'm so sorry, Leeland. I wanted to be there for you, wanted to be strong. We're friends, and I know how hard it is to be my friend, how weird I am, how patient you are, the things you do for me, with what you put up, but I just couldn't watch, couldn't see you get hurt even though I know you're strong, that you can take it, that you know what you're doing. I'm so pathetic. I can't be your friend, because what friend would just close his eyes and hide in Martin's chest while you're out there on the battlefield?"

Collin started sobbing. Jonathan threw a curious glance at Martin. The man was clearly suffering with his sub but did nothing to soothe him. Instead he looked at Leeland, who simply nodded. Leeland grabbed the shaking Collin and dragged him onto his lap.

"Hey, hey, sweetie, calm down. I'd thought you know me better by now. When did I ever give you the impression you're not exactly the kind of friend I need and want?"

Collin hiccupped against Leeland's chest.

"Collin, do you remember when we first met? At that barbecue at Martin's house?"

Collin nodded.

"What did I tell you back then?"

"That Tim Burton is a genius?"

Leeland chuckled. "Apart from that."

Collin sniffled. "That we're all crazy. That's why we fit."

"Exactly. Now, what makes you think your special brand of crazy is suddenly not fitting anymore?"

Collin fisted his hands in Leeland's dark green shirt. "But I couldn't watch!" He sounded as if this was the worst offense he could think of.

Leeland made a tsking sound. "You tried. That's all that matters to me. Not everybody is wired the same way. You don't like seeing me getting hurt. Actually, I like that. It means you care about me, love me. What more could I ask for?"

At those words Collin sat up. There was a sliver of hope on his tear-streaked face. It almost broke Jonathan's heart, seeing the brilliant artist like this. Collin was way too fragile for this world. It was painfully obvious how much he needed a keeper. Jonathan glanced over at Martin, who watched the interaction between their boys with rapt attention. It couldn't be easy, taking care of somebody as sensitive as Collin, though Martin didn't look as if it was a hardship for him. *To each their own*, Jonathan thought fondly. He loved both Collin and Martin like brothers. They were a part of his extended family, and he was glad they could handle problems like this one openly.

"Me loving you is enough?" Collin still sounded timid.

Leeland kissed him on the nose. "Of course, silly. We're good. You've been great ever since I started my crazy training schedule, and you saved me more than once from losing my shit because of sugar deprivation."

At the mention of sugar, Collin turned beet red and pressed his index finger on Leeland's lips. "Shh, that's supposed to be a secret!" he whispered loud enough for Martin and Jonathan to hear. Jonathan raised a brow, but Leeland only shrugged.

"You haven't heard a thing."

With a smile, Jonathan mimicked closing his mouth off. Now that the crisis seemed to be averted, he couldn't help but notice how beautiful the two subs looked together, hugging each other in a tangle of long, graceful limbs. The way Martin was adjusting his crotch none too subtly told Jonathan he was aware of it as well. Leeland shot them a knowing look before he turned his attention back to Collin.

"You just keep taking care of me like you did and everything's perfect. I have Dean, Curtis, Emilio, and Peyton who can come to the fights. There's no need for you to get worked up over it. That's what having a family means—everybody does their best in their own way."

Collin nuzzled Leeland's neck, a happy smile lifting the corners of his mouth. "I never had a family, so I guess I'm learning while I go along. I'm glad you're part of my family. This is great. Thank you, Leeland."

"You're welcome, sweetie."

Next to Jonathan, Martin shifted and cleared his throat. "Very well. Now, baby, do you want to sit on my lap for a bit?"

Jonathan grinned when he heard the slight strain in Martin's voice. The imposing Dom was as troubled as he was by the sight of their beautiful boys together. Collin, as almost always, was oblivious.

"I'd rather cuddle with Leeland some more, Martin. This feels so nice." He beamed proudly at his master, snuggling closer to Leeland, which gave Jonathan all kinds of interesting ideas, none of which could be implemented right now, much to his dismay. "I'm his family!" Collin added with a hint of pride in his voice that had Martin smiling, if a bit strained.

Over Collin's head, Leeland stuck his tongue out at the two Doms and winked. Jonathan shared a look with Martin, and they silently agreed to make their boys pay for this later.

CHAPTER 12

Three months later

LEELAND SANG along to Gloria Gaynor's "I Will Survive" on his way over to Curtis's house. It was their boys' night, and he was looking forward to meeting his friends. The last two times they had met, he'd been too tired. He had been in—and won—two more fights since the first one against Carlos. His ojisan, Greg, and Samantha were ecstatic, all of them doubling his workload to get the maximum out of his current high flying. As it turned out, he attracted a different clientele than the people from Smash! had initially hoped for, but they didn't look a gift horse in the mouth. The blogger from his first fight, Leandra Donnell, had started following him after her blog about his fight, and the interview had been met with overwhelming interest. Apparently women did have a thing for fighting, if it was done with a certain style and came in an appealing package. Leeland always stayed true to himself, never slighting his opponents before or after a match. He was the picture of politeness and manners, and many people loved him for it—as much as others hated him. He had been given the nickname Prince because he was so different from all the other fighters with their macho posturing and openly shown violence.

Leeland wasn't too happy about all the attention he was getting, though so far his sexual orientation hadn't been discovered and his ojisan's charity was thriving. After a public training session where he worked with the kids in the program, donations for Hinode had increased. Apparently Leandra's followers—for she had hosted a live feed of the event—loved the charity. All in all, things would be going well if it weren't for Noah Adams, Leeland's next opponent in the octagon. Their match was scheduled in a week, and Leeland wasn't looking forward to it. Noah Adams was the very picture of a homophobic macho who lived for insulting others and seemed to be completely ruled by his own warped perception of manliness. It was his second year in the UFC, and so far he had yet to lose a match. For reasons only plausible to Sean Shelby, Noah hadn't fought for the championship belt last year, a fact that seemed to gnaw at him, for he did everything to get media recognition, which in turn increased his chances to get nominated for the championship fight. His tactics also included calling Leeland a sissy boy, an effeminate faggot, a spineless cocksucker, and other slurs on Twitter and his Facebook page. Disgusted by the hateful rhetoric, Leeland had stopped paying attention to the rants. He knew Samantha kept a close eye on it, but as long as Noah ranted under the guise of simply garnering attention for the match, nobody would do anything against it.

Leeland sighed. There was no such thing as bad PR. At least not in the world of UFC.

The ringing of his phone tore him from his musings. He smiled when he saw the caller ID. Pressing the button on the steering wheel that allowed him to take the call, he greeted the man on the other end of the line.

"Hello, Carlos! It's good to hear from you."

"Hello, Leeland. I just wanted to see if you're good."

Since their fight, Leeland and Carlos talked at least once a week about their training and the misery of being on an athlete's diet. He truly liked Carlos, and Carlos seemed to take great pleasure in talking to him. Carlos's trainer, Mason, was also his stepfather and a true dick. If he ever found out Carlos and Leeland were talking, he would probably kill them both. He didn't believe in sportsmanship or friendship, only in winning and being the strongest, an opinion Carlos didn't share, which led to regular fights between the two men. Thankfully Carlos had won his last two matches as well, which had mellowed Mason a bit.

"I'm very good. I'm on my way over to a friend's house for movie night and pasta."

Leeland grinned at the mention of Mamma's pasta. It had taken him forever to have his ojisan and Greg concede to him eating a normal meal tonight, but he had won.

"You're allowed pasta only one week from your next fight?" Carlos sounded disbelieving. "How did you manage that?"

"I told them I'd go crazy if they didn't let me have empty carbohydrates and bad fat."

"And?"

"They told me to grow a pair. I did just that and pestered them until they would do anything just to shut me up."

"Wow. Congratulations, man. I envy you. It's another night of chicken breast and broccoli for me."

"Sorry to hear that. Have you tried chopping your almonds, roasting them, and then putting them over the broccoli? It's almost tasty when you do that."

Carlos sighed. "I did. And you're right. The broccoli is a bit better with the crunch. Unfortunately I already had my ration of nuts with my shake today. Never try to mix spinach with almond butter, by the way. It's warfare to your taste buds."

The gagging sounds coming through the phone had Leeland laughing. "Poor thing! And thanks for the advice. I don't think I would have tried mixing these two, but now I definitely won't. Tell you what, I'm going to eat some delicious white-wheat pasta with creamy sauce just thinking of you, okay?"

Carlos whined over the phone. "You're cruel!"

"Am not!"

"You so are!"

They both started laughing and it felt good, liberating. Carlos was the first to sober up.

"I wanted to wish you good luck with your fight against Adams. Be careful. That man's a major asshole. I've seen what he's been posting, and I can't believe the UFC is letting it happen."

Leeland sighed. "It's the usual posturing before a fight. Well, a little more than that, but it's getting them attention. Attention equals screen time equals money. And let's be honest, this isn't about you, or me, or Adams, or even the sport. This is about money. Pure and simple."

Leeland knew he sounded bitter, but he couldn't help it. The world of professional sports was a toxic environment at best. Given the image the UFC had chosen for itself, it was no wonder Noah Adams's verbal attacks were smiled upon rather than punished, as if he were an adolescent testing his limits instead of a fully grown homophobic asshole who had crossed the line into open, unfiltered hostility a long time ago. Civility and manners had no place in the UFC.

"That's awful. Just awful." Carlos paused. "Sometimes I wonder if it's worth it. All the stress, the crazy eating habits, the reflexive lashing out at everybody. I mean, we no longer live in caves, but seeing some of our fellow athletes, I could be fooled."

"Not all people can be as cultured as we are, Carlos."

Leeland wanted to lighten the mood, and given how Carlos chuckled, he had succeeded.

"No, probably not. I'm sorry to cut this short, Leeland, but I've to get my chicken breast and then some much needed downtime. Enjoy your evening out and good luck with Adams. You can beat that idiot."

"Thanks, Carlos. I'd say I wish you fun with your meal, but we both know that's a lie… so have a nice, relaxing evening. I'm looking forward to our next call!"

"Me too, Leeland. 'Bye."

"'Bye."

The line went dead. Leeland took the last turn to Curtis's house, his thoughts already on the food he was soon going to eat.

CURTIS OPENED the door to his tasteful little villa with a smile on his face. Even though Leeland knew he could easily afford a home as grand as that of Richard or Martin, Curtis preferred his sanctuary a little south of downtown Miami. He had bought the house after his disastrous breakup with Jasper O'Malley, the asshole Dom who'd dumped him for a younger model three years ago. Leeland remembered well how devastated Curtis had been and how much it had cost him to rebuild his life without the worthless piece of shit. When it came to Jasper O'Malley, none of the subs had a good word to say. It wasn't just the way he had treated Curtis, although that was the main reason, but also how he acted as a Dom. O'Malley was a man who never understood the true concept of submission, and how Curtis had ended up with the asshole in the first place remained a mystery to Leeland. He suspected the saying was true and love was indeed blind.

"Hello, Leeland! We're all so glad you could make it today!"

Curtis smiled at him warmly, and Leeland sank into his embrace that smelled faintly of the expensive cologne Curtis used.

"I'm glad too. Now, where's the food?"

Curtis chuckled. "I thought that would be the first thing on your mind. It's already here. Collin said he wanted to bring somebody new today, but we don't have to wait. He understands your need for pasta."

"The doll. Let's go."

Leeland knew he was being a bit rude, but the prospect of getting tagliatelle and spaghetti and fusilli in his ravenous stomach had him drooling a little. He just couldn't wait any longer. The moment he entered the dining room—in that respect, Curtis was a lot stricter than Collin—he was overwhelmed by the delicious smell of Mamma's best dishes. Dean, Peyton, and Emilio were already waiting for him, Dean wordlessly handing him a plate with a selection of his favorite pasta. Leeland choked out a "Thank you" before sitting down. His fingers actually trembled in joy when he twirled the first mouthful of spaghetti on the fork. He knew the orgasmic groan he made when the food landed in his mouth was porn-worthy. There was nothing like real food. His athlete's diet was no doubt better for his body and physical health, but his soul yearned for things that had nothing to do with healthy or wholesome and everything to do with taste. When he became aware of the silence around him, Leeland looked up from his plate.

Dean smiled at him, Peyton just rolled his eyes, and Emilio busied himself with preparing his own plate.

"I can't tell you how delicious this is." Leeland's smile felt broad enough to cut his face in half. He was in heaven.

"We know, Leeland, we know. And you deserve every single bite."

Dean sounded a bit like he was trying to calm a crazy person down. Leeland huffed and stuck his tongue out.

"I'm not dangerous. Just starved."

"Which is the same," Peyton intervened. "The only thing worse than you deprived of food is Emily on a sugar high, and only because her voice can reach a higher register than yours."

Since his tongue was already used to the fresh air, Leeland showed it to Peyton as well. Before he could come up with a sharp retort—he was kind of distracted by the pasta on his plate—they heard the doorbell again.

"That would be Collin and his mysterious guest," Dean murmured while Curtis got up to answer it.

Expectantly, they all eyed the door through which the men would be entering. Curtis appeared first, an unreadable expression in his eyes. Then came Collin, and behind him a redhead about six feet tall. Collin grabbed the man's hand and dragged him toward the table.

"Hi, everybody, this is Seth Redmond. I met him in the wild, and he's real cool and nice and as crazy as we all are, but different, and he's going to be my wedding planner, and I hope you all like him because I think he's perfect for the job."

Leeland watched Seth Redmond carefully during this breathy introduction. He wore a white T-shirt that showcased a well-defined chest and healthy biceps covered in colorful ink. Dragons, flowers, and tribal patterns made for a very intriguing picture. His slim waist and long legs were covered by the tightest pair of leather pants, his eyes highlighted with black eyeliner. Seth Redmond looked like a cross between a bad boy motorcycle club member and a high-maintenance twink, but somehow, he managed to rock the look. His red hair was artfully tousled on top, the sides a bit shorter, and the freckles on his skin added to his appeal. He was looking at Collin with a dazed expression that was common upon first exposure to Collin. Leeland extended his hand.

"Hi, Seth. I'm Leeland Drake. Nice to meet you."

Seth took his hand, the smile on his face crinkling the corners of his eyes. If pressed, Leeland would guess the man was in his thirties, though he couldn't be sure.

"Nice to meet you too." He had a warm, deep voice that projected calm and kindness. Leeland liked it.

Peyton got up from his chair. "Hi, I'm Peyton, and this is Dean. Are you really a wedding planner?"

Seth raised a brow at the blunt question but answered nevertheless. "Hi, Peyton, Dean. Yes, I am a wedding planner. I know I don't exactly look like one, but—"

Peyton cut him off with a gesture. "You look perfectly fine. Don't worry about that." He turned to Dean, hand outstretched. "You owe me twenty, mister."

Dean grumbled while producing his wallet. Seth seemed like he didn't know what to make of this and looked at Collin, who just shrugged. Leeland had a suspicion what this was about but wasn't sure. It was Emilio who enlightened them.

"They had a bet going. Peyton said Martin would find a wedding planner soon, while Dean was convinced he would get fed up with all the drama, whisk Collin away to Vegas, and marry him there without any of us present."

Collin gasped. "You think Martin wanted to do that?"

"Well, he did seem a bit skittish to me last time I saw him over at our place. I thought he was getting ready to bolt." Dean grinned, showing Collin that he was making fun of him. Though with Dean, the difference was hard to tell. Leeland loved the man like the brother he never had, but he could be a terrible tease sometimes.

Collin reached over the table and slapped him lightly on his upper arm. "Martin wants a wedding here, with all his friends and family present."

"Exactly what I told him!" Peyton chimed in.

"Ha! If I remember correctly, *you* said something about Olivia shooting Martin in the knees if he dared to elope. No talk of love and family." Dean looked indignant.

Peyton shrugged. "The wording doesn't matter. The outcome is what counts," he announced triumphantly.

Leeland turned to Seth, who still stood rooted on the spot. "Welcome to the asylum. This is actually pretty tame, so if you want to run, now is your chance." He winked at Seth.

Seth shook his head like a kitten that had gotten wet. "No. I think I like it. Anyway, it was Collin who brought me here. I kind of expected things to be... different."

"Spoken like a true diplomat." Curtis gestured toward the empty chairs around the table. "Please, take a seat and help yourself to some food. We have a nice selection of Mamma's pasta dishes, a Merlot to go with them, and sodas if you prefer something nonalcoholic."

Seth inhaled. "Smells delicious. Thank you, I'll take a mineral water. I still have to drive today."

Curtis nodded and poured him the beverage. When they all had filled their plates, Peyton looked at Seth with puckered lips. "Now, Seth, tell us everything about you, and start with how you met Collin here."

Seth took a sip from his water and looked at Collin, who was busy slurping down his spaghetti carbonara. "It's a strange story, but you probably already guessed that."

Leeland couldn't suppress a chuckle, just like the others.

"I was out going on a jog on one of the trails in the glades when I heard somebody talking. I looked around, and suddenly the biggest, meanest-looking rottweiler I've ever seen appeared on the trail. I almost wet my pants." Seth shuddered. Emilio made a sympathetic noise in the back of his throat, and Curtis reached out to pat Seth's hand reassuringly. Dog could be a bit intimidating when you didn't know him.

Seth took a bite of his pasta. After chewing, he caught Collin's gaze and winked. "So there I was, not knowing if I'd live to see the evening. Me and the dog were having an honest-to-God staring contest, when suddenly I heard someone squeal, 'Dog, they're coming, they're coming!' The rottweiler took off, and after a moment's hesitation, I followed."

Peyton clucked his tongue, which caused Seth to grin. "I know. Not my smartest move. What can I say, I'm terribly nosy."

"Just who do you remind me of…?" Dean wondered loudly enough to have Peyton punch him on the arm.

"Anyway, a little off the path, I found the dog next to a man who was staring at something on the ground with rapt attention. I went closer, and the man looked up at me and said, 'They're finally coming out. I've been waiting forever since I saw how busy the hill was. Look, all those princesses, getting ready to fly off on their wedding. Aren't they beautiful?' With that, he looked back at the anthill, where indeed a lot of ants with wings were crawling around. Then I noticed the sketch pad and could finally make a *little* sense of the situation."

Seth smiled, clearly enjoying the memory. "I've never given anthills much thought, apart from not wanting them in the garden or house. I watched Collin sketching for about an hour, and I just couldn't bring myself to leave."

Leeland reached out to pat Seth on the arm. "Happens to the best of us. Especially when Collin is around. He has that effect on people."

Seth nodded. "I figured. When the last princess had taken flight, we started talking about insects in general and ants on their mating flights in particular. Collin told me he's going to be married and, well, one thing led to another. Now here I am."

Leeland was still thinking about how funny coincidences could be when Curtis reached out to get the last of the *spaghetti alle vongole*, which caused Leeland to fly into action. "Mine!" he yelled more fiercely than intended.

Curtis seemed a bit startled but withdrew his hands and held them up in a soothing gesture. "It's okay, Leeland. Nobody is going to steal your food. Right, guys?" Curtis looked around the table, where Leeland saw his friends nodding furiously. Even Seth, whose puzzled look would have made Leeland laugh if it weren't for the gravity of the situation. This was food, precious, delicious carbohydrates with saturated fats and even a hint of alcohol in the *vongole*, and sharing just wasn't an option, not after the months he'd had to go without. Leeland winced. And the months still to come. Tonight was an exception. He had to make the best of it.

Dean took pity on Seth, who did look a bit confused, and explained. "Leeland is currently a professional athlete in the UFC and on a strict diet. He has somehow managed to convince his trainers to let him off the hook for tonight, which means he's trying to consume his weight in pasta and create sugar reservoirs for the next five months."

"You're an MMA fighter?" Seth looked at him wide-eyed. "I'm kind of a fan, though for the last year, I wasn't able to follow the matches. Moving here and setting up business had me working all the time."

"I'm just filling in for somebody. My uncle has a gym, and his fighter broke a leg. In order to keep his sponsor, my uncle had to find a replacement. No big deal."

"Oh, but it *is* a big deal!" Peyton chimed in. "So far Leeland has won all his fights. He's that good."

Leeland didn't know whether to feel annoyed or not. He didn't like bragging, probably because of his Japanese heritage, though his mother wasn't fond of it either. His parents had taught him accomplishments had to be made, not talked about. Peyton, on the other hand, believed firmly in giving credit where credit was due. And it felt good to be praised by his friend. Still—

"I was lucky."

Seth raised one of his perfectly plucked brows. "Somehow I doubt that, but I'm going to watch your fights on the internet and form my own opinion. Wow, this is so cool! I get to meet a UFC fighter!"

Seth's unbridled joy had them all laughing. They ate the rest of their meal bantering happily back and forth. When Leeland had licked the last bit of tiramisu from his bowl, Curtis led them into his spacious living room. Each of them found their favorite spot on the large, whiskey-colored, U-shaped couch in front of the flat-screen on the wall.

"What are we going to watch today?" Peyton asked, dread shining in his eyes.

An evil smile appeared on Curtis's face, causing Peyton to flinch. "I thought we could venture into the world of sci-fi tonight." He made an ominous pause, during which he pinned Peyton with a deadly glare. Leeland knew that look. Curtis was daring Peyton to bitch about his choice of film. These two had a movie feud going that was a source of never-ending entertainment for Leeland and the other subs, even though they sometimes had to suffer through exceptionally bad movies.

"*Blade Runner* with Harrison Ford and *The Island* with Ewan McGregor."

Peyton threw a pillow in Curtis's general direction and missed. "You ass! You were taunting me on purpose!"

Curtis flicked some invisible dust from his lilac button-down shirt. "Who was threatening me with a Dwayne 'The Rock' Johnson marathon the last time we met? Who? Oh, I think that was you, Peyton. A joke in bad taste if ever I heard one. This is payback, and don't you forget it!"

Peyton pouted. "Fine, I apologize. That wasn't the nicest thing to do. In my defense, I had a shitty week and needed to unwind."

"You don't unwind like that." Curtis shuddered. "The Rock," he added, lifting one of his brows.

Leeland elbowed Seth, who was sitting to his left. "Since I have a feeling you're becoming a regular in our little group, you need to learn the rules—there are none."

When Seth glanced at him in question, Leeland elaborated. "Whoever hosts the evening gets to decide which films we watch. As you may have guessed, our tastes vary greatly. You can always choose to antagonize the others by selecting something horrible, which is fun for you, on your night. Just remember, their turn will come as well."

"I get it. I'd like to sign up as last on the roster. That way I can get a feel for what you guys enjoy."

"Have fun with that," Dean murmured to Leeland's right before snuggling into him. Leeland sighed contently. With carbohydrates and sugar in his belly, his friends around him, and a good movie playing, he could ignore the looming threat of his fight against Noah Adams.

CHAPTER 13

JONATHAN COULDN'T believe it. Two minutes into the fight with Noah Adams and the obnoxious asshole had already gotten three fouls in, of which the referee had only seen one. Jonathan hoped the judges weren't as blind. In the last two days before the fight, Noah's verbal bullshit had become so bad, even Jonathan couldn't listen to it or read it anymore. He had followed the man on Facebook, Twitter, and the media to be able to shield Leeland from unexpected surprises. But when the threats against his boy grew more personal with each post and tweet, Jonathan had to make a choice. He could either keep on reading and listening and call Martin afterward to have the fucker removed from the surface of the earth, or he could stop and concentrate on supporting his boy. After long, careful consideration, during which he was tempted to go with option number one, Jonathan finally decided to focus on Leeland. His lover had been tense the days before the fight, more so than before the other matches he had competed in. When Jonathan asked him about it, Leeland explained what was going on in his complex mind. "It's just—he's nasty, Jonathan. He's not just posturing and ramping it up for the fight; he really believes what he says. I can feel it. And I can't lose against such an ass. No way."

Jonathan understood. He understood very well. So he'd done everything in his power to help Leeland get ready for his meeting with Noah. And now here they were, Noah going full-speed right from the beginning, waling into Leeland as if he wanted to use him as a punching bag. He'd clearly thought he could end the fight within the first few seconds, sending Leeland down with one heavy blow. The idea that Leeland could put up a fight and even have the audacity to gracefully duck out of the way didn't seem to have occurred to Noah, because he was obviously getting angrier with every jab Leeland evaded and every kick Leeland got in. Red as he was in the face,

Jonathan wondered what would happen first—Noah blowing a blood vessel or starting to froth.

The whistle sounded and the first five minutes were over before this question could be answered.

Jonathan watched his lover retreat into his designated corner with concern. Leeland had taken some bad hits from the asshole, and Jonathan could only hope adrenaline was keeping the pain at bay for the moment. Later he could take care of his boy, could kiss all his hurts better. The thought distracted Jonathan for a moment and had him smiling until Martin elbowed him.

"Next round!" his friend hissed.

Jonathan glanced to his right, where Martin, Richard, Dean, Curtis, and Emilio were seated. They always made sure some of them were with Leeland to show him their support, and Richard and Martin hadn't missed a single fight. They were almost as proud of Leeland as Jonathan himself and paid for any extra amenities Smash! wouldn't grant Leeland, such as a suite with a Jacuzzi and a personal attendant. Jonathan could have afforded giving these luxuries to his boy, but Richard and Martin always insisted, though they had no problem with Jonathan paying his share of the rooms they booked.

Routa and Layla Drake weren't there today, both working on cases that demanded their full attention. They had talked to Leeland via Skype before the fight, wished him good luck, and given him some last-minute fighting advice.

Suddenly the crowd roared, dragging Jonathan's attention back to the fight, where he saw Noah staggering backward. The way Leeland was gracefully lowering his left leg to the canvas suggested he had just performed a high kick and found his mark. Noah roared. Even from the distance, Jonathan could see the fury shining in his eyes. He ran toward Leeland, fists raised, clearly wanting to get him square in the face and obviously not caring—or realizing—how stupid that move was. As Jonathan had expected, Leeland sidestepped and sent Noah forward with a vicious elbow strike to his rib cage. But Noah managed to spin around quicker than Jonathan would have thought he could. This time he got Leeland with a hammer fist to the ribs that Leeland couldn't block entirely. Knowing how painful this particular method of striking an opponent was, Jonathan grabbed the sides of his chair so hard his knuckles were shining white. He hated seeing his boy, his lover, getting hurt, especially by a scumbag like Noah Adams.

The whistle sounded again, announcing the second sixty-second break in the fight.

Noah stomped over to his side of the ring, cursing and spitting like a rabid dog. He was bleeding from a cut above his left eye, and his pale skin was glowing in different shades of red where Leeland had hit him. Through his short, light brown hair, Jonathan could see sweat glistening on his scalp. Leeland was definitely forcing him to give this fight his all, and Noah clearly resented the way things were going. Given how he had boasted about sweeping the floor with Leeland, Jonathan wasn't surprised.

Leeland was slumped against the cage, his chest heaving, while he drank some water from the bottle Greg was offering him. He, too, was bleeding from a cut below his hairline, the blood trickling slowly toward the bridge of his nose. Misaki was wiping the blood away and tending to the cut while talking urgently to Leeland, and Jonathan would have loved to know what he was saying. But he couldn't be down there, couldn't be close to his beloved boy, and he resented it deeply. Only the knowledge that this was a temporary arrangement meant to protect Leeland kept him from running over to Leeland's side and showing him his support in a more direct way.

Too soon the break was over, and Leeland and Noah met in the middle of the octagon for the last five minutes. Noah's body language showed how agitated he was, trembling with barely suppressed rage, while Leeland appeared to be completely calm, which made Jonathan's chest swell with pride.

The referee stepped back, and again Noah tried to end the fight with a quick, hard punch. His movements were slower than at the beginning of the fight; the many kicks and blows Leeland had gotten in had to be taking their toll. Leeland didn't move with his usual quick grace either. Both fighters acted as if they were drunk, stumbling around more than executing controlled attacks. Some of the audience started booing, not impressed with the turn the fight had taken. Jonathan was only worried about his lover. In all the fights before, Leeland had never looked so sluggish. Noah must have hit him more severely than Jonathan had thought. The only consolation was that Noah didn't look good either. Since neither Leeland nor Noah were any longer in a condition to throw effective punches or kicks, they went into a clinch, each man trying to get into a position where he could take his opponent down or force him into a submission hold. Jonathan watched with worry as Leeland tried to keep his balance when Noah Adams attempted an ankle hook, while at the same time, Leeland twisted his hips in order to throw Noah on the mat. Both men looked as if they would fall over any second, and Jonathan wondered why the referee didn't end the match.

He breathed a sigh of relief when the whistle finally marked the end of the fight. Leeland and Noah tumbled back, both panting heavily. Leeland braced his hands on his knees, and Jonathan saw blood dripping on the mat between Leeland's feet. His heart yearned to get down to his boy, take him in his arms, and make all the hurt go away. Of all the hardships Leeland's time as a pro had brought with it, Jonathan found this was the worst—not being able to be where he belonged. At his boy's side.

Since both opponents were still standing, and the referee hadn't ruled one of them out with a technical KO, the decision of who would be named the winner lay with the judges. After a few agonizing minutes, during which the three men did the calculations on the points they had deducted during the fight, they signaled the outcome.

It was a draw.

Jonathan wasn't sure how to feel about that, because at the moment he was overwhelmed with clashing emotions. Relief that the fight was over and Leeland wasn't too badly hurt. Worried about the hits Leeland had taken. Glad he hadn't lost against this unpleasant opponent. Angry because the referee hadn't seen all the fouls Noah Adams had committed.

Noah Adams, on the other hand, didn't seem to have the same problem. He roared in anger, threw his balled fists up in the air, stepped around the referee, and screamed something in Leeland's face that Jonathan couldn't understand over the ruckus the audience was making, some of them booing, others whistling and cheering. Leeland just slightly bowed his head in the direction of the judges, completely ignoring his raging opponent, once more showing his class, which became even more apparent next to the snarling, spitting Noah Adams. Even though the entire fight felt wrong to Jonathan, he was proud of his boy and the way he carried himself in this difficult situation.

The referee backed the still-shouting Noah into his corner of the octagon while Greg and Misaki approached Leeland and led him to his changing room. Jonathan felt a stab in his heart at not being able to follow them. He had to wait at least two more hours until all the interviews were done—probably more, given how the crowd had reacted. He felt a pat on the shoulder and turned around to see Martin standing behind him.

"We're out of here. Let's go back to the hotel."

Jonathan nodded his agreement. At the entrance to the arena, Richard's limousine was already waiting. When he sank back into the soft leather seat, Jonathan had to admit being friends with a billionaire had its perks.

"This whole fight was a total sham!"

Curtis was the first to speak his mind. To Jonathan's surprise, the distinguished British gentleman had quite a violent streak. He also knew a lot about boxing, since this was apparently a sport even the upper crust in Britain enjoyed, and he had therefore quickly immersed himself in the world of MMA.

"I don't understand why the referee didn't end the whole thing. I mean, this Adams character committed more fouls than I've ever seen. That the referee didn't see them all, I can understand, but the judges? By any rights, Leeland should have won, even with this stupid scoring system." Dean sounded uncharacteristically aggressive, something Jonathan attributed to all the testosterone flying around in the arena.

"It's fine, baby. I think nobody really understands the system they're using." Richard stroked Dean's back soothingly.

Jonathan rolled his eyes. No, nobody understood that system. The judges were there as a kind of backup when a fight didn't end with a clear winner—like tonight. For each round, a fighter started out with ten points, from which the judges deduced some for fouls, timid fighting, bad style, or whatever else they didn't like. To Jonathan the

system seemed as bad as the scores in figure skating or gymnastics—
two sports he didn't watch for that exact reason.

"They should be forced to explain every point they deduct or
not. With all the fouls this Adams guy made, he should have gotten
negative points." Dean was obviously not in the mood to calm down
or let go of what he seemed to think was a valid point. Even when
Richard pulled him into his lap, he kept on ranting under his breath
about how unfair it all was, encouraged by Curtis, whose opinion
of the system was equally low. They were already close to the hotel
when Martin suddenly held his hand up.

"Shh, the interviews have started."

Immediately they all shut their mouths. Martin turned up the
volume on his smartphone, with which he had found the live feed
from the press conference. The first voice they heard was that of Noah
Adams, who worked himself into a rage right at the first question.
With every word he spoke, his voice got higher, which made him
sound more like an angry pig than the manly stud he normally tried
to project. Not that he had any success, in Jonathan's opinion, but he
sure made one hell of an effort.

"Mr. Adams," Jonathan heard a reporter ask, his voice slightly
distorted through the speakers on Martin's phone, "what do you think
about the decision of the judges?"

"Total bullshit! I mean, you all saw this fight! I was clearly the
one in control, not sissy boy with his beautiful hair. If this were a
hairdo contest, he would have stood a chance, but no, this is the UFC,
not 'find the beauty queen,' and there's no way I haven't won against
this little cunt."

Jonathan felt anger rise inside him when he heard Noah's insults.
Personally he found Leeland's hairdo for the fights beautiful—he
braided his silky long hair into four cornrows close to his scalp,
combining the strands to one when they reached his neck, which he
then slung into a bun at the base of his skull.

Somehow the reporter managed to get another question in
before Noah worked himself into an epileptic episode. Even though
Jonathan could only listen to the interview, he had seen enough of
them to picture what was going on. His only consolation was the hope

that Noah would collapse from working himself up before he could spew any more hatred. As it turned out, there was no such luck.

"So you're saying the judges are wrong, Mr. Adams?"

"Damn right they are! Stupid motherfuckers. How anybody could see that fag boy as equal to me and my fighting skills is beyond me. They had no right to call this a draw. That man is not a fighter, he's some pretty little boy, and my guess is the judges liked the shape of his ass. Nothing else explains their decision."

On and on it went, insult after insult, many of them homophobic slurs, even though nobody knew yet about Leeland's sexual orientation, until finally the live feed was cut off. After listening to Noah, Jonathan prayed Leeland's being gay would stay a secret until he dropped out of the UFC. The idea of what people like Noah Adams, who seemed more than content to use anti-LGBTQ phrases to insult others, would do once the truth was out made him shiver. Any athlete who exposed him- or herself to this type of hatred deserved to be sainted.

The calm voice of an announcer informed the audience they would now switch to Leeland Drake. When Leeland's melodic timbre filled the car, Jonathan felt his heart swell. Only he could tell from the slight trembling on some syllables how agitated his boy was. In that moment Jonathan wanted nothing more than to be at Leeland's side. It was a feeling he was becoming all too familiar with.

The reporter asked the same questions Noah Adams had answered, though the difference between the two answers couldn't have been greater. Where Noah had ranted like an angry bull, Leeland's replies were measured and polite.

"Mr. Drake, what do you think about the decision of the judges?"

"Well, it was certainly not what everybody had expected, but I trust them to be fair and know what they're doing."

"It seems as if Noah Adams doesn't share that sentiment."

"I can't speak for my opponent. When I signed the contract with the UFC, I knew the rules and accepted them. It's no use musing about what-ifs. Things are the way they are."

The interviewer tried a few more times to get a more violent reaction from Leeland with carefully phrased questions, which Leeland answered as shortly as possible and always avoided sounding hateful or angry. He definitely lived up to his nickname, and Jonathan pictured him holding court like a real prince. The image had him smiling.

Finally the reporter gave up. While they had been listening to the interviews, the limousine pulled up in front of their hotel. They got out and bid each other good night. Jonathan hurried to the suite Richard had booked for him and Leeland. He took a quick shower before he sat down in front of the huge TV, flipping through endless channels without seeing what was on, waiting for his lover to come to him.

WHEN LEELAND finally arrived, he was so exhausted he could barely stand. Jonathan swooped him up in his arms to carry him to the bed.

"You were so good tonight, honey."

Leeland buried his nose in the crook of Jonathan's neck, a gesture that made goose bumps appear on Jonathan's naked back.

"I didn't win." Leeland sounded half-asleep.

"You didn't lose either, and with an asshole like Noah Adams as your opponent, that means a lot."

"Uhm-hmm."

Jonathan didn't try to get any more words out of his boy, simply put him on the bed, took off his clothes, and then snuggled in behind him.

This was how things were supposed to be.

CHAPTER 14

LEELAND WOKE to the wonderful smell of omelets and pancakes. He stretched luxuriously on the bed, basking in the scent of Jonathan that clung to the sheets. As a reward for the fight against Noah Adams, his ojisan had given him an entire week off. On second thought, this had probably less to do with Misaki wanting to be kind to Leeland and more with Leeland being too sore to even think about training. Noah Adams's fists were hard. Leeland had spent the first three days of his holiday commuting between their bed, the couch, and the bathtub, while eating everything he had been denied for the past months. He knew he would pay the price for his binge eating when he had to go back to training, but at the moment he couldn't care less. Jonathan had taken the week off as well, to pamper him to the best of his ability. Leeland didn't complain. His master was an expert at spoiling him and loved to show off his skills.

Leeland left the bed to follow the enticing smells from the kitchen. When he entered, he found Jonathan standing at the stove, flipping pancakes. The sight of his Dom's muscular back in a tight black muscle shirt, wielding the spatula like a pro, had his cock hardening in his pajama pants. This was his man, his lover, preparing breakfast for him. Leeland was no doubt the luckiest man on earth. And the horniest.

As if he had somehow sensed the indecent direction Leeland's thoughts were going, Jonathan turned around, a bright smile on his face.

"Good morning, honey! How do you feel today?"

Leeland smiled back, full of love. "Good morning to you too, Master. I'm feeling a lot better. The bruises hardly hurt anymore."

For a moment Leeland saw a shadow cross Jonathan's features. Apparently his Dom had a hard time seeing him injured.

"So you're up for something else besides lazing on the couch today?"

The teasing tone immediately woke Leeland's interest. "Why? Do you have something planned?" He couldn't help the sultry tone that crept into his voice.

Jonathan grinned, as if he had an inkling what Leeland was thinking. "It could be that I made some plans for today, but only if you feel well enough."

"Oh, I so do feel well enough!" Leeland meant every word. "Are we going to Whisper?"

"Not today, no." Leeland pouted and watched Jonathan raise a brow. "We'll go there at the end of the week. I want you to be one hundred percent when I have my wicked way with you."

The lascivious tone had Leeland's entire body screaming for hot, rough sex, right here, right now, and pancakes be damned. Jonathan winked, obviously knowing exactly what was going on in Leeland's mind.

"Patience, honey. It's supposedly a virtue."

"Not in my book. So if you don't plan on fucking me over the kitchen table, what are we going to do?"

Jonathan laughed out loud. "I love your directness. It's like a breath of fresh air. First, we're going to eat our omelets and pancakes. I made chocolate chip ones. After that—a surprise."

"What? Come on, Jonathan, you know how bad I am with surprises! The suspense is going to kill me before I can have a bite of the pancakes, and wouldn't that be too bad?"

Jonathan hummed. "We're going outside." He raised a finger. "I'm not telling you more, boy."

He was using his stern Dom voice, so Leeland knew better than to keep wheedling. Instead he sat down and enjoyed his breakfast.

When they were done, they did the dishes before Jonathan led Leeland back into their bedroom.

"Put on your leather gear. We're going for a ride."

Leeland felt giddy with joy upon hearing those words. Riding with Jonathan was among his top five things to do. In fact, it ranked third after cuddling with his master and having hot, kinky sex with the man. He slipped into his tight black leather pants, the matching boots, and a black tank top before putting on his black leather jacket—why ruin a good color scheme when you had one? Jonathan had done the same and took his hand. Together they went downstairs through the garage, where Jonathan's mechanics were working on obscenely expensive cars and bikes, making them even more valuable. Why people would invest so much money in what essentially was an assortment of metal pieces and bolts was beyond Leeland. He fell firmly in the "it's got a motor so I can use it to make my life easier" category, but since Jonathan made quite a lot of money by tinkering with cars and bikes, he never complained.

The mechanics greeted them with grunts and halfhearted waves, too engrossed in their work to acknowledge their lazy boss and his boyfriend. Leeland loved the rough openness Jonathan fostered among his employees. It made for a great working atmosphere one could feel when entering the shop.

They passed through to the side, where another garage housed Jonathan's two cars and his precious collection of motorbikes. Even though he was blessedly clueless about motorcycle brands and the pros and cons of different kinds of bikes, Leeland did have a favorite, a huge black beast of a Harley whose vibrations practically forced him into Jonathan's broad back during each ride. It was this bike Jonathan rolled out of the garage. He straddled the leather seat—black, of course—and patted the pillion seat.

"Hop on up, boy."

Grinning happily, Leeland complied. Jonathan reached back to hand him one of the two helmets that had been dangling from the handlebars before putting on his own. Leeland did the same. Then he slung his arms around Jonathan's waist, snuggling as close to the broad, muscular back as possible. The leather added a nice, arousing tone to the whole situation, and Leeland knew he would be hard as nails by the time they came across the first traffic light. Jonathan turned the ignition and the Harley roared to life. Leeland caught their reflection in the window of one of the shops they were passing.

"Man, we look like impending doom," he stated through the intercom in his helmet. Jonathan turned his head to see what Leeland was referring to, then started chuckling as well.

"Yeah, we do. Or as if we have to compensate for something…."

"Hey, black is a perfectly acceptable color. Goes with everything. We never have to worry about our outfits not matching. And leather… well, leather is perfect for riding a bike."

"I agree with you one hundred percent, honey. You were the one who said something about 'doom.'"

Leeland made a kissing sound that had Jonathan rumbling with approval.

"Now that we're out on the street, can you tell me where we're going?"

"You really are impatient, boy. Perhaps I should teach you some manners… tie you up and leave you hanging, not letting you come, put a blindfold on you… ohhh yeah, sounds delicious."

Leeland's grip around Jonathan's waist became like a vise. He felt his muscles going tense with the strain. "You tease! You know what it does to me when you talk like that!"

"Yes, boy, I do know. I'm just kindling the fire for the day after tomorrow, when we go to Whisper. I'll give it to you so good then. Mmm-hmm."

"If you keep doing this, there won't be a fire because I'll jump you the moment we get off the bike."

Leeland felt Jonathan's back go rigid. He was apparently very much on board with that idea.

"Stop tempting me, boy."

"You started it!"

Before their argument could turn into a toddlers' shouting match along the lines of "You!", "No, you!", Jonathan set the blinker, turned left on Collins Avenue, drove on for a few more minutes, and finally pulled up in front of the Miami Beach hotel. Leeland hopped off the bike, opened the visor of his helmet, and looked at Jonathan for an explanation. He had nothing against a day at the beach, but why would Jonathan park at a hotel?

With a grin, Jonathan got off the bike as well. He took Leeland's hand and marched him into the lobby. If the receptionist was surprised to see two leather-clad bikers walking in, she didn't show it.

"Hello, gentlemen. What can I do for you?"

Jonathan flashed her a smile. "I have reservations for a spa day. The name's Jonathan White."

"One moment, Mr. White. Ah, here you are. Yes, the Luxury Package. I assume this is Mr. Leeland Drake?"

"Yes."

She smiled. "Welcome to the Spa at the Miami Beach. Here are the cards for your lockers. You can leave everything in the changing room. In your lockers you'll find bathrobes, the swim shorts you requested, and flip-flops. Tina at the spa reception desk will show you around. We have a juice bar, water is available from drinking fountains, and you can use the sauna and pools the entire day. Tina will inform you when and where your massages and other treatments take place. Have a lovely day at the Spa, gentlemen."

Stunned, Leeland accepted one of the locker cards from her perfectly manicured hands. They started walking in the direction of the spa, indicated by a huge sign.

"That's the surprise?"

Jonathan glanced at Leeland. "Yes, the first part. Do you like it?"

"Do I like it? Jonathan, this is great!" Leeland hesitated. "You know you don't have to spend that much money on me?"

Jonathan slung an arm around Leeland's shoulders and pulled him close, which made walking a little awkward.

"I know, honey. But I wanted to do it. You're under a lot of pressure at the moment, and I want you to relax and to reassure you that we're good. That our relationship stands strong, even when we aren't doing much regarding kink."

Leeland had to blink back the tears that were threatening to spill. Instead he stopped and went up on tiptoe to kiss Jonathan on the mouth.

"You know me so well. Thank you, Jonathan." Leeland rubbed his cheek on Jonathan's. "And if you ever wonder if you're doing this relationship thing right, let me tell you, you're more than good at it. Perfect, I'd say. I know how hard this is for you, and I can't express with words how much it means to me that you're there for me. I love you, Jonathan."

"And I love you, honey. We're in this together." Leeland felt Jonathan's lips graze his forehead. "Now let's go. On Dean's recommendation, I booked us two different massages, a facial treatment, and a pedicure."

Leeland lifted his brows. "A pedicure?"

Jonathan shrugged. "I always wanted to know how those feel."
Giggling, Leeland followed Jonathan into the spa.

AT THE end of their spa day, Leeland was so happily relaxed, he thought he would fall off the bike during their ride home. The massages had been great, especially the belly massage, but the best had been the pedicure. Leeland didn't know what magic the nice man possessed, or how he knew just where to press to release all the tension Leeland hadn't even been aware of, but this was definitely not his last appointment with Jules. Leeland thought he was levitating, it felt so good. It almost seemed as if the stairs leading up to their apartment didn't exist.

Jonathan sent him to change while he made a phone call before joining Leeland in the bedroom.

"How do you feel, honey?"

"Relaxed, boneless, happy. Thank you, Jonathan. This was a great idea."

"I'm glad you approve. Originally I wanted to take you out to a fancy dinner afterward, but I think we're both too tired. I just ordered from Mamma's. We can eat on the couch, watch a movie, and cuddle to our hearts' content. How does that sound?"

Leeland pressed his pajama-clad body against Jonathan's leather outfit.

"Like the perfect end to a perfect day."

Jonathan leaned in to kiss Leeland. It was sweet and slow and so full of love, Leeland felt tears of joy streaming down his cheeks. He was home and happy.

CHAPTER 15

SMILING, JONATHAN watched as Leeland was snatched by the subs at Whisper the moment they came through the door. It had taken them the entire previous day to get over the deep relaxation their trip to the spa had brought them. Jonathan probably wouldn't admit it out loud, especially not to Richard, who was quite vocal about his dislike of spas, but he could definitely see the allure in being pampered senseless. And his skin was baby soft from the scrub that had been part of one of the massages. Leeland had already commented on the new feel often enough for Jonathan to know he would be booking another treatment soon.

They had come to Whisper early to give Leeland a chance to reconnect with the other subs and listen to their problems before they would retreat to one of the private rooms for a scene. Tomorrow was Leeland's last day as a free man before he had to start training again. Jonathan wanted him to use that day to laze around and them both to simply enjoy each other's company.

"Your boy's in high demand." Martin's voice sounded amused while they both watched as Collin flung himself at Leeland like an overexcited puppy.

"They don't get to see him as often as they used to. I can relate."

Martin placed his left hand on Jonathan's shoulder. "I know this must be difficult, Jonathan. I don't think I can imagine how big a change that must be for you."

Jonathan pried his gaze from Leeland to look Martin in the eye. "Not harder than living with a genius, I guess."

Martin chuckled. "You got me there." He turned serious. "How are you two holding up?"

Jonathan sighed. "To be honest, it's not as bad as I thought it would be, though not as good as I wish. Leeland is under a lot of pressure, from himself, his uncle, Smash!, and even me. He's too much of a perfectionist to not give this thing his all, even though he's supposed to be just an emergency replacement. Sometimes I suspect Misaki was counting on Leeland's competitive streak. And as soon as the people from Smash! realized he can win, they started increasing the pressure. They're still pretending to be all nice about it, but even I can feel their expectations."

"What about you? As far as I can tell, you're his pillar of support. How are you pressuring him?" Martin asked quizzically.

"That's the thing, I don't. It's in his head. Because this whole thing is so hard on Leeland, he thinks the same goes for me. Which, of course, is true to some extent and adds to the pressure he already has. He somehow thinks our relationship is in danger."

"And is it?"

"Strangely enough, no. When he started training and I finally realized how strenuous it was going to be, I thought I would panic. You know me, Martin. Leeland is my first steady relationship in ever. By any rights, I should have freaked out. But I didn't. Perhaps it's because I know this is temporary. There's a definite end to Leeland's stint in the UFC, which makes it easier to deal with the whole circus."

Jonathan glanced at Leeland, who was standing amid his friends close to the bar, laughing and accepting hugs from them. "And even if it weren't temporary, I'd still support him fully. It's the one thing I've learned in the last few months—Leeland is it for me. I can't imagine being with anybody else, even if that suited my lifestyle better. I want to be there for him, help him, love him, face it all with him, the good and the bad. Because without him, even the good feels kind of bad."

After that emotional statement, Jonathan avoided Martin's gaze. It wasn't normally his style to open up to somebody else like that. Being with Leeland had changed him a lot. Next to him, Martin turned and offered him his hand. Jonathan stared at it, puzzled, before he finally looked into Martin's dark eyes. The man grinned like a madman.

"Welcome to the club, Jonathan. You're now officially as whipped as Richard and me. If I remember correctly, Garrett calls us the 'sap club.' It's nice to have a new member."

Jonathan tried—and failed—to keep his laughter in. He took the offered hand to shake it in the manliest way possible. He knew Martin was right, but he could still try to preserve some of his dignity.

"Why do you let Garrett get away with it?"

Martin shrugged, a mischievous glint in his eyes. "Richard and I, we see the signs. If I'm not completely mistaken, the strict Master Garrett is on his way to succumbing to the lure of a certain sub with hazel eyes and dark brown hair. It's only a matter of time, and I'm a patient man."

Both Jonathan and Martin looked at the sub in question, Emilio, who was laughing about something Leeland had said. The boy looked different from the first time Jonathan had met him. He knew Emilio was training with Garrett, and it was starting to show impressively. Emilio's chest was broader, his arms more heavily muscled than only a few months before. The new look suited him, at least in Jonathan's opinion.

"How did Leeland deal with the end of the last fight?" Martin sounded concerned now. It reminded Jonathan how much the burly co-owner of Whisper cared about Leeland and how invested he had become in his career.

"The bruises are healed, though it took longer than after the other fights. What truly got to him was the nastiness that is Noah Adams. Leeland isn't used to that kind of toxic masculinity and has a hard time dealing with it. Unfortunately, that's one of the things I can't completely shield him from." Jonathan squared his shoulders. "But I have every intent of showing him tonight what real masculinity is all about."

"What have you planned, if I may ask?"

"A *shibari* scene. I need to remind Leeland that he's safe with me. That he can trust in our relationship and let himself fall, because I'm there to catch him."

Martin clapped him on the shoulder. "You're a good Dom, Jonathan. A good man. I'm glad to call you friend."

"You just want me to pimp your new car, admit it!"

They both grinned, somewhat relieved to leave their emotional exchange behind.

"Did it work? I'm hoping for a substantial discount here."

Jonathan just huffed and flipped Martin the bird before he started walking toward his boy.

IT TOOK some effort to get Leeland away from the other subs, but Jonathan finally managed by putting on his best "scary Dom" face. If some of the bolder subs tried unsuccessfully to hide their snickers, he pretended not to notice. Jonathan led his boy to the private room he had booked, happy anticipation coiling in his belly. When he opened the door, he felt Leeland stiffen.

"Master," he whispered. "It's beautiful."

Jonathan smiled happily. That was exactly the reaction he had been going for, and whoever of the Whisper staff had prepared the room for them was in for a hefty tip. Thick white candles burned on almost every flat surface, illuminating the room with a soft, intimate glow. The padded bench he had requested stood in the center, the black leather gleaming invitingly. To the right, on a small table, were the deep red, silken shibari ropes promising sensual pleasure for both of them. Jonathan pulled Leeland close to kiss him on his temple. That was not exactly high protocol, but tonight wasn't about doing things by the book. It was about doing things right.

Jonathan started unbuttoning Leeland's simple black shirt, taking his time, enjoying how his boy's breathing synchronized with his own, how they both started panting the closer he got to the last button. Then the shirt gaped open, revealing Leeland's smooth skin. Jonathan trailed his fingers along the cloth, noticed with satisfaction how goose bumps appeared on his boy's skin, followed the path upward where he slid his hands under the shirt to push it over Leeland's shoulders.

"So perfect, boy."

Leeland whimpered softly, leaning into Jonathan's touch, just as it was meant to be. For what felt like an eternity, Jonathan stroked Leeland's naked upper body, reveled in the connection the simple act of touching brought him, before he traveled back down to the fly of Leeland's leather pants. The first button popped open, and Leeland's hips jerked forward into the touch. Jonathan smiled, satisfied by the reaction. This was what he wanted, Leeland giving him everything without thinking about what was appropriate.

"My beautiful boy, my honey. So good."

"Master."

Leeland grabbed Jonathan's upper arms. The contact sent a shiver through Jonathan, right down to his cock. He hastened to open the remaining buttons and to get the leather pants off Leeland, suddenly eager to start their game. As soon as Leeland was naked, Jonathan guided him to the padded bench.

"Lie down, boy."

Leeland obeyed with half-lidded eyes, already emitting that erotic aura Jonathan could never resist.

"Close your eyes, boy."

When Leeland obeyed, Jonathan took the first coil of rope from the table and let the soft fabric graze Leeland's skin. His boy shivered in anticipation. Jonathan took Leeland's left wrist and started wrapping the rope around it.

"Just let go. All you have to do tonight is feel. The ropes, my hands, your pleasure. This is about us, about who we are. You can always trust me to have you, to hold you, to love you no matter what. I'm here for you, Leeland."

Jonathan watched a single tear slide from his boy's eye, trailing down his cheek as Leeland obviously struggled with the deeper meaning behind those words. His beautiful lips parted, no doubt to argue with Jonathan.

"Shh, boy. This is a no-brainer. You're mine as much as I'm yours. Trust me like you always do. We've got this. I've got this."

"Jonathan!" A shudder ran through Leeland's slim, yet perfectly toned frame. Then he relaxed visibly, melting into the padding on the bench, silently—finally—accepting what Jonathan had to offer.

"Oh, honey, you're so perfect." Jonathan slung the remaining length of the rope around Leeland's left ankle, before he went around the bench to do the same with his boy's right side. Now Leeland's legs were spread, displaying his slim, elegant cock and balls to Jonathan's hungry gaze. Jonathan took another, shorter piece of rope and slung it around Leeland's cock and balls, effectively trapping his boy's erection in a makeshift cock ring. Leeland moaned deep in his throat.

Jonathan stepped between Leeland's spread legs. His hands skimmed over the inside of Leeland's thighs, making his boy quiver in anticipation. Then Jonathan leaned in to breathe the heady scent of Leeland's arousal. A glistening drop of precum had already formed at the tip of his boy's cock, glittering in the light of the candles. Jonathan breathed on it, which sent a shiver through Leeland's body.

"Master." It sounded like a cross between an order and a plea.

Jonathan smiled.

"Open your eyes. Look at me."

When Leeland complied, Jonathan kissed the cockhead, then sucked the precum into his mouth. Leeland bucked his hips.

"Enjoy, boy. Just tell me when you're getting close. Want to be inside you then."

Leeland groaned. "Yes, Master."

Satisfied with this answer, Jonathan started to work on his boy. First he licked his whole length, swirling his tongue over the slit where more precum was leaking. Then he went down on Leeland's balls and sucked them into his mouth, one after the other, and massaged them with his tongue until Leeland squirmed so badly under him, he had to steady him with both hands.

"God, Master! So good!"

Jonathan grinned and let the heavy orbs go. He grabbed Leeland's asscheeks to expose his pretty pink hole. Jonathan loved rimming Leeland; it gave him a strange sense of utter power when he felt his boy squirming under the assault of his tongue. He started with slow, long licks over the wrinkled skin up to the wet, glistening balls. When he dabbed his tongue against the tight outer ring of muscle for the first time, Leeland howled. He was now leaking copious amounts of clear liquid. His hips jerked in an attempt to get closer to Jonathan's tongue, and Jonathan loved how completely undone his boy was coming.

He rolled his tongue and darted the tip past the sphincter into Leeland's wonderful heat. Jonathan felt his own moan rise in his throat as he tasted his boy. Leeland was the sweetest drug he knew, the best thing he'd ever tasted.

"Master, close!"

Jonathan immediately withdrew from Leeland's delicious hole to give his boy a chance to come down from the edge. Jonathan didn't want this to end too soon, and judging from the hungry look Leeland was giving him, his boy was with him. As soon as Leeland calmed down, Jonathan started his assault again, only to withdraw when Leeland warned him. He did it two more times before his own erection was so hard, he couldn't ignore it any longer. Jonathan opened the fly on his leather pants to free his cock before he reached for the bottle of lube on the table, squirted a generous amount on his fingers, and started opening Leeland while sucking the tip of his cock at the same time. Since Leeland always reacted very well to rimming, it didn't take Jonathan long to have him stretched enough. Panting, Jonathan aligned his cock with his boy's hole. They gazed at each other while Jonathan slowly sank inside Leeland's tight heat.

"So perfect. My boy, my honey."

"Master. Jonathan. You. Only you."

Even though the things they said were hardly coherent, Jonathan knew exactly what his boy was telling him. And somehow, deep in his heart, he knew Leeland understood him just as well. He moved slowly in an attempt to draw things out, to make this physical part of their connection last as long as possible. Leeland clamped down on Jonathan's cock as if he wanted to do the same. Jonathan loved how in sync they were at this moment. Nothing besides them mattered; it was just him and the love of his life.

Despite his wish to remain inside his lover like this for the rest of eternity, Jonathan felt the telltale tingling in his balls as well as the flex of Leeland's abdominal muscles that told him how close they both were. Jonathan quickly undid the rope around Leeland's cock before he started a more punishing rhythm. His boy urged him on with moans and pleas for more and harder. After only a few more thrusts, Jonathan felt Leeland stiffen beneath him. Warm liquid coated both their stomachs. Knowing that he had pushed his boy over the edge, that he had pleased his lover, ignited Jonathan's own orgasm. With a roar he emptied himself into Leeland's spasming channel, let his boy's body milk him for the last drops of his cum. Insanely satisfied, Jonathan collapsed on top of Leeland. As if he hadn't gotten the memo that they were completely done, his cock kept on twitching hopefully inside Leeland. His boy groaned.

"Feels good."

"Mmpf." Jonathan was the first to admit that was pretty lame, even for postcoital talk. Leeland chuckled, which sent vibrations through his entire body. When they reached Jonathan's cock, it finally calmed down and slid from its wet, sloppy paradise.

"So good, Jonathan. I love you."

Jonathan kissed Leeland deeply. "I love you."

He got up, took some of the wet wipes from the table, and cleaned first himself and then his boy. After that, Jonathan undid the ropes, helped Leeland from the bench, and carried him to the king-size bed for their aftercare. Once they were settled in, Leeland flush against Jonathan's body, a blanket over them both, his boy looked up at him.

"Thank you, Jonathan. I needed this. And I'm sorry."

Jonathan raised a brow. "For what?"

Leeland's cheeks flushed pink. "For not trusting in us." He made a vague gesture with his hand.

Jonathan caught him by the wrist to kiss each knuckle on his hand. "You did trust in us, honey. All you needed was a reminder that I'm as serious about our relationship as you are. I don't blame you, Leeland. I know I'm not an easy man and given my history…."

Leeland rose far enough to kiss Jonathan on the lips, effectively shutting him up. "I'm so glad I found you. It feels so good—to let go, to rely on you. As for the 'not easy' part—who is? What Dom would have asked me out after learning that I'm not as submissive as I seem? What Dom would have stayed with me, been proud of my skills, even if others might see it as a weakness? What Dom would have supported me through this madness that is the UFC? Only a great Dom could do it, and it so happens I have the best of them all!"

The cheeky smile on Leeland's lips made Jonathan burst out in laughter.

"My sweet, sweet honey. I think we were made for each other."

"Yeah, custom-made, like one of your cars."

They both chuckled, content and happy. Jonathan started stroking Leeland's naked back until deep, regular breathing told him his boy had fallen asleep.

THEY SPENT the next day happily lazing on the couch, making out in the sweetest way, and watching mindless shows on TV. They ordered takeout from the Chinese restaurant two blocks from their apartment, eating in the living room while the TV was still on. To Leeland, that was the height of depravity, as Jonathan well knew. Apparently Leeland's parents had both been adamant about not eating on the couch, much less watching TV at the same time. Most of the time, Leeland still followed those rules unconsciously unless Jonathan actively went against them, like now. It felt good, being in their home—which was gorgeous, even if Jonathan would never admit that to Peyton, ever; the man was conceited enough as it was—together, just enjoying their deep connection.

Of course nothing that good could last forever.

They had just agreed on watching *Sweeney Todd* before going to bed, when Leeland's phone rang. With a sigh Leeland heaved himself up to retrieve the cell from the small table in the hall where he usually placed it when he was at home. Jonathan watched his boy come back with a serious expression on his face and raised a brow in question. Leeland held up his free hand.

"Wait a minute, Ojisan. I think Jonathan needs to hear this as well. I'll put you on speaker."

Leeland lowered the phone from his ear, pressed an icon on the screen, and put the cell on the coffee table in front of the couch.

"You're on speaker now, Ojisan."

"Thank you, Leeland. Good evening, Jonathan."

"Good evening, Misaki. You have something to tell us?"

Jonathan hated how worried his voice sounded, but Leeland was so tense, it made Jonathan's internal alarm shrill like crazy.

"Yes, indeed." Misaki sounded calm enough, a fact that didn't fool Jonathan. Misaki *always* sounded calm. It had something to do with his Japanese upbringing. "I received two calls today, one from Samantha, one from the UFC. Both are—complicated."

Jonathan hated how Misaki was dancing around the topic, something Leeland had explained to him was normal behavior for the man. Since he didn't want to be rude to his lover's godfather, Jonathan took a deep breath, reminding himself that patience was a virtue. Leeland, on the other hand, didn't seem to feel a need to restrain himself.

"Ojisan! Just tell us already! I have a film waiting for me."

A deep sigh came through the phone speaker, as if Misaki was trying to find the courage for what he had to tell them. It didn't help Jonathan to calm down at all.

"The UFC informed me that you will be fighting for the championship in two months. Your opponent will be Noah Adams."

"Fuck!"

Leeland voiced what Jonathan felt. They both would have been happy to never see Noah Adams again. It seemed the gods of MMA— or more precise, Sean Shelby—had different plans. When Jonathan thought about it, he could even understand why. Both Leeland and Noah had a clean record of wins with one draw—from the fight against each other. Nominating the two would make for great PR, especially since their characters were so different and Noah was so good at generating attention in the media. From a purely economic point of view, this match was a wet dream, with countless opportunities to make money and get PR for the UFC. Sean Shelby was a genius.

"That is not all."

The slight trembling in Misaki's voice alerted Jonathan. If having to fight against Noah Adams wasn't the worst-case scenario, then what was?

"Samantha called as well. It seems as if somebody saw you two at a hotel in the Keys three days ago. There's a picture of you kissing, and it's already all over social media. I'm afraid you're the first male athlete to come out in the UFC, Leeland."

For a moment none of them spoke. Jonathan looked at Leeland, who had gone very still, his eyes trained on the phone as if he wanted his uncle to take the words back.

Regret tinged Misaki's voice. "I'm so sorry, Leeland. I'm going to hang up now. Samantha wants to talk to you first thing tomorrow. She wanted to call you the moment we realized what was going on, but I told her to leave you alone. Try to get some rest and don't worry too much. We'll deal with this."

The connection broke.

Jonathan opened his arms, and Leeland stepped into his embrace with a sigh. After a few minutes of cuddling, where Jonathan got the impression his boy wanted to crawl into him, Leeland finally spoke. His voice sounded muffled against Jonathan's chest.

"Fuck, fuck, fuck. Why couldn't they find out after the match? Or never? It's bad enough I have to fight against Noah Adams—again. I don't want to deal with all the other shit that's surely coming our way."

Jonathan pressed a kiss on Leeland's head. "It's okay, honey. We knew this could happen. We've come this far. We won't let this stop us now."

"I hope you're right, Jonathan. I have a feeling I'm in way over my head."

"Oh, honey, maybe. But I'm here with you. You're not alone."

"Thank you." Leeland squirmed in Jonathan's arms until his back pressed against Jonathan's front, which had Jonathan's cock immediately interested.

"Do you still want to see the film? Or do you want to go to bed?"

Leeland snuggled into Jonathan, and the sad tone in his voice broke Jonathan's heart.

"I think I still want to see the film. Nothing like some blood and gore to take my mind off this mess."

CHAPTER 16

Two weeks later

"MR. DRAKE, one moment please! How do you feel about—"

Leeland hurried to get into Jonathan's Volvo and thanked the gods and his car-loving boyfriend for tinted windows. Once he was inside the car, nobody could take pictures of him, which was a relief. The dual announcement of him being gay and fighting Noah Adams had generated even more publicity than Leeland had feared in his worst nightmares. Of course Noah had sunk his teeth into the information immediately, and there was no sign he would let go of it anytime soon. If Leeland hadn't stopped checking social media in general and Noah's Twitter rants in particular before their first fight, he would have now. Jonathan only told him the bare minimum of what he had to know, and it wasn't pretty. The nicest thing Noah had said about him was how it was no wonder the judges had ruled a draw in their fight, because they had smelled the gay on Leeland and hoped for a piece of ass. That he was also insulting the judges didn't seem to register in his little homophobic brain.

To say Leeland's outing had made some waves in the UFC was like saying it was a little chilly in the Arctic. All the big news channels had picked up on it, and if Leeland got a dollar for every athlete, former athlete, trainer, friend of a trainer, sports manager, and sponsor who felt obligated to add their ten cents to the topic, he would be a rich man. Though there were many UFC athletes who took Leeland's side, the haters seemed to feel it was time to air their homophobic feelings, even though most of them had had to apologize for antigay comments before. The fact that Noah Adams could rant as much as he wanted without getting more than a light verbal slap on the wrist gave them the courage to join him.

Leeland knew Dana White's restraint on the topic wasn't necessarily to do with him being antigay and everything with the media coverage the UFC was getting out of this. And as long as White rebuked Noah Adams for the things he said, he was on the safe side. Several LGBTQ-rights groups, bloggers, and magazines were already asking for harder sanctions, thus drawing even more attention to the championship match in six weeks. If White played his cards right—which meant not punishing Noah for his hateful rhetoric by withdrawing him from the fight—he could elevate the UFC to new heights of popularity.

Intellectually, Leeland understood that. Business came first. And it wasn't as if Samantha wasn't milking the whole situation for Smash! as well, but he still felt betrayed. Being an athlete in a major sport should mean he would be protected against the hatred and bigotry not only of other athletes, but also from the fans. As it was, he needed Jonathan and his friends as his safety net and source of support; otherwise Leeland would have given up by now. The only other reason he wasn't seriously thinking about quitting was that he didn't want Noah to have that triumph. Leeland had his pride.

Still lost in thoughts about how unfair and toxic the whole situation was, Leeland started the car. He winced when he put his foot on the brake, his sore muscles protesting loudly. Now that they had the championship in their sights, his ojisan and Greg had intensified the training even more. Nobody pretended it was enough if Leeland simply showed up for the fights anymore, which was kind of a relief. To Leeland's own surprise, he found he was better able to deal with the expectations of his ojisan, Greg, and Smash! now they were expressing them openly. The unspoken demands had pressured him more than the open ambition.

Leeland steered his car through the afternoon traffic back to their apartment. Fortunately there were no paparazzi waiting for him there. When the bomb had first gone off, they had been everywhere, like cockroaches. They had even tried to get interviews with Jonathan, but his man had put on his scary face and driven them away. He had also put a restraining order in place to keep journalists from sniffing around the garage, although Leeland thought it was more fear of the mostly heavily muscled, gruff-looking mechanics that kept the vultures at bay than anything the law could to do to them.

Leeland drove into the garage after opening the gate with a remote control Jonathan had put in the glove compartment, parked the car, got out, and climbed the stairs to his safe haven. When he opened the door, he was greeted by the smell of food. His heart did a happy little jig in his chest. His man, his Dom, was cooking for him. Jonathan had started doing the cooking shortly after the media scrutiny had begun. Leeland suspected it was because Jonathan knew how pampered he felt when somebody, especially Jonathan, took care of him. It was a nice break from their usual routine—though Leeland did enjoy preparing meals for Jonathan—and it helped Leeland to deal with the madness his life had turned into.

He wandered into the kitchen, where Jonathan was just setting the small table.

"Hello, gorgeous." Leeland couldn't help the seductive purr in his voice. Somehow, Jonathan brought out his horny side every time he laid eyes on him.

"Hello to you too, honey. Did you have fun at the gym?"

Leeland made a face. "If you call being trained as if I were a slave and then being harassed by the media again having fun, then yes, I had fun."

"Poor baby." Jonathan put a kiss on Leeland's forehead. "I wish I could tell you I made your favorite food to make it all better, but all I have is a delicious broccoli salad with some almonds and, believe it or not, chicken breast!"

They stared at each other, and this time Leeland was the first to start laughing. It was a game between them, one of the many things that helped him cope with the stressful situation. They tried to make light of all the things he had to endure, and it helped. Not as effectively as a carton of ice cream and his favorite chocolate bar to spoon it out with, but it was still better than nothing.

"So I'll take the chicken breast. I'm sure it's—tasty."

"You bet it is! I tried something new with chili oil and ginger."

"Sounds like fun."

"Oh yes, it is. And you know what? Tomorrow it's tilapia with brown rice! Isn't that great?"

Leeland made a face. "Wonderful, Master. I can't wait for tomorrow."

Jonathan swatted his ass with the dish towel before they sat down to eat, and it wasn't as bad as Leeland had feared. Jonathan was a decent cook; he just preferred to hide it. After the meal, they took a bath together, another ritual that helped Leeland to relax. Once they were out of the water, Jonathan gave Leeland a full-body massage with arnica oil, and if he hadn't been so bone-tired, Leeland would have taken full advantage of it. As it was, he fell asleep halfway through.

THE SUN was shining through a gap in the curtains when Leeland woke. Judging from the angle of the rays, he knew it had to be early still. He didn't know what had woken him; he certainly felt like at least two more hours of solid sleep were required before he could get up to deal with yet another day of merciless training and intrusive reporters. Jonathan was gone, and for reasons Leeland didn't understand, he felt a chill through his body. Something was wrong. Terribly wrong.

Leeland dragged himself out of bed. He made a quick trip to the bathroom before he went into the hall. From the kitchen he heard Jonathan's deep voice talking to somebody. He sounded upset. Did they have a visitor this early? Leeland stepped into the kitchen, and the look on Jonathan's face while he was talking on the phone had him frozen on the spot. His man looked devastated and worried and freaked out. Not a good combination.

"Leeland has just woken up. I need to talk to him now."

Jonathan ended the call. Leeland took some hesitant steps toward him. He could feel the blood draining from his face.

"Who is it? My mother? Father? One of my friends? Oh God, not Dean!"

Leeland started trembling as he imagined all the horrible things that could have happened to his loved ones. He felt strong arms around him, and the soothing presence of his lover engulfed him.

"Shh, honey. Nobody is hurt. Last night your uncle's gym was vandalized and set on fire. Nobody was in it at the time, but it's a total loss. The police are already on it since it was obviously arson. They could smell gasoline everywhere. On the walls of the neighboring buildings, there's antigay graffiti, so it was probably a hate crime. This is not your parents' precinct, but they have friends on the force who are doing everything in their power to find out who did this."

First Leeland felt a great wave of relief wash through him. Nobody he loved was hurt. That was wonderful. Then he felt anger, quickly followed by fear. His stomach turned to ice. Nobody he loved was hurt. But they could have been. Setting fire to a building was serious. People could have been injured. People could have died. He could have lost—

"Leeland! Stop it! I'm here, darling. I'm here. Just breathe. With me. In and out. In and out."

Jonathan's voice pried Leeland from his panic, and he realized he had started hyperventilating. He needed to calm down. Following Jonathan's example, he started taking deep breaths, releasing them slowly by counting to five. After several breaths his limbs stopped trembling and his heart rate went back to normal. Gently, Jonathan steered him into the living room, where they sat down with Leeland on Jonathan's lap. They kept on breathing together, Leeland taking in his lover's calming scent. When he felt a little better, he leaned back from Jonathan's broad chest to look at him.

"What happens now?"

Leeland felt the pad of Jonathan's thumb stroking over his cheek in a featherlight touch.

"Needless to say, training is canceled today. I just spoke with Misaki. He'll be busy talking to the police, insurance, the people from Smash!, the media. He said you should try and relax a bit."

Leeland couldn't suppress a bitter laugh. "How am I supposed to do that?" He felt a sob working its way up his throat and tried his best to keep it down. "Somebody burned my ojisan's gym! And for what? Why? Because I'm gay? Because he helps kids from the street? Because somebody didn't like the color of Greg's skin? Why?"

"Shh, honey. The police are going to find out. There's not much we can do at the moment, so I thought, if you want, we could call your friends. Ask them if they want to come over. If you think that will help. If not, we just hole up here and have all kinds of sex the entire day."

Leeland hiccupped and chuckled at the same time, which made for a strange sound.

"As much as I'd love for you to fuck my brains out, I think having my friends over, watching stupid movies, and eating as much sugar as possible would be better for me. I need to process and cope, and I can't do that with your dick in my mouth or hole. Somehow my brain always shuts down when that happens."

Jonathan laughed out loud and pulled Leeland back into his arms. "You're a delight, do you know that?" He extricated Leeland's arms from around his neck, much to Leeland's dismay, and gently sat him on the couch. Leeland looked up into his man's beautiful, rough face and marveled once again how he could have gotten so lucky.

"I'm calling Dean. Once he hears what's happened, I bet he's here in a flash."

JONATHAN WAS in the kitchen, dialing Richard's number. Leeland had decided to take a shower before his friends came. After only two rings, Richard answered the call.

"Jonathan. What's up?"

Jonathan sighed. "I need help."

"What happened?"

For a moment Jonathan allowed himself to close his eyes and thank the gods for a friend like Richard.

"Misaki's gym was vandalized and set on fire last night. As you can imagine, Leeland is devastated. Do you think Dean could come over?"

"He'll hop into the car the moment I tell him. Does Leeland want to see only Dean, or his other friends as well?" As always, Richard showed caution and consideration.

"Honestly, I think the more the better. He needs to process it, and the boys will help give him a sense of stability and normalcy."

Jonathan listened to himself for a moment and started chuckling the moment Richard did.

"Okay, normalcy in their own very special way. Does that sound better?"

Richard snorted. "Any sentence with 'the boys' and 'normalcy' in it is kind of ridiculous." He turned serious again. "But they will be there, which is the only thing that counts. With your permission I'm going to talk to Martin as well. We need to discuss security measures for both you and Leeland. I don't want to take any risks."

Jonathan hadn't even thought that far ahead yet, but now that Richard mentioned it, he realized how much danger they both could be in. "Thank you, Richard. This means a lot."

"You're welcome, Jonathan. You know I consider both you and Leeland family. I'll call you back later."

A beeping sound told Jonathan that Richard had ended the call in his brusque "there's things that need to be done" way.

About an hour later, after Jonathan had managed to get some fruit into Leeland, who tried his best to put up a brave front and was failing miserably, the doorbell rang. He went to open it and found Dean and Collin at the front door, both carrying huge, heavy-looking bags. Dean opened his mouth to greet Jonathan when suddenly his eyes went wide and he stepped forward, ignoring Jonathan completely. Jonathan turned his head to see Leeland standing in the hall, looking lost and desperate. Without hesitation Dean went to his friend, pulled him into a tight hug, and whispered so softly Jonathan almost didn't hear him. "Oh, sweetie, I'm so sorry."

It didn't take more. The thin veneer of bravery Leeland had managed to uphold until now cracked, and Leeland broke down sobbing and crying like a small child. Jonathan was glad. His boy needed to let it all out. He could have probably achieved the same result with a scene, but Jonathan instinctively knew it was better this way, with Leeland's friends present to remind him that he wasn't alone in this.

Collin handed Jonathan the bags they had brought before he went over to where Dean and Leeland were hugging. He joined them, slinging his arms around both the other men, nuzzling his face into Leeland's neck. They stood for some time until Leeland's sobs ceased. When he seemed to have calmed down, Dean leaned back a bit and smiled at him.

"We brought all your favorite ice cream and chocolate. The others will be here soon. All we have to do now is hole up in your living room and start the sugar feast."

Leeland sniffled. "Great idea. I could use some sugar."

"Oh, it's not only *some* sugar. When this day is over, you might not want to see something sweet for the rest of your life."

Dean sounded somber, as if he meant every word. Jonathan couldn't hide a grin. Dean's sweet tooth was almost as bad as Leeland's. The two were brothers in sugar and chocolate. Seeing how his boy slowly started to relax, Jonathan carried the bags into the kitchen to inspect the contents, though he doubted it would be worth the trouble of putting the ice cream in the freezer. It wouldn't have time to melt once his boy and his friends started digging in.

CHAPTER 17

CURTIS AND Peyton arrived next, carrying even bigger bags than Dean and Collin.

"I didn't know what you had in your kitchen, so I brought everything for chocolate chip pancakes, cookies, and lava cake," explained Curtis with that polite expression of his that always made Jonathan feel a tiny bit like a hick. The man was the very definition of a British gentleman in every gesture he made, every word he spoke.

"Less talking, more action. Let's go see Leeland and find out what he wants first."

Peyton, on the other hand, was refreshingly blunt. Now that the man was done redoing his apartment, Jonathan actually enjoyed seeing him.

"They're in the living room. If you hand me the bags, I'll take them to the kitchen."

"Thank you, Jonathan. That's very kind of you." Curtis handed him the bags before he and Peyton went into the living room.

The boys were still discussing whether to make chocolate chip pancakes or cookies first when the bell rang again. This time it was Emilio and a man Jonathan didn't know but thought he recognized from Leeland's description. After greeting Emilio, who acted as shy as ever, Jonathan held his hand out to the stranger, who put down a large box he had been holding before shaking Jonathan's hand.

"You must be Seth, Collin's wedding planner. I'm Jonathan White, Leeland's—partner," he ended after hesitating for a moment. Jonathan assumed Seth had to know about the special kind of relationships that Collin and most of the others had, but it always paid to be careful.

The redhead smiled at him. "Nice to meet you, Jonathan. Forgive me for being so blunt, but Leeland is your boy, isn't he? Collin mentioned something like that."

Jonathan nodded. So Seth knew and seemed to be okay with it. "Yes, Leeland is my boy. And my lover."

Seth grinned. "Collin has also told me you customize cars and restore old-timers. Would you mind giving me your card? Sometimes couples request special transportation for their weddings."

A bit taken aback by this business request, Jonathan rummaged in the bowl on the table in the hall where he and Leeland kept their keys and everything that needed dropping after walking through the door. He finally found one of his cards. The corners were a bit ragged, but the most important part, his contact information, was clearly visible.

"Here you go."

Seth beamed at him. "Wonderful! Thank you." All of a sudden, his face fell. "I'm sorry. This was terribly rude of me. Asking for your card when you surely have other things to worry about at the moment. Sometimes I get carried away."

Jonathan patted Seth on the back. "Don't worry. If I had thought your request was inappropriate, I would have said so. You startled me a bit, but not in a bad way. Now go into the living room. If you hurry, you can give your opinion on pancakes versus cookies."

"Why would there be a discussion?" Seth seemed to be truly confused, and for a moment Jonathan doubted if this newcomer fit as well into Leeland's group of friends as Leeland's stories had made him think. But Seth's next words put all of Jonathan's worries to rest. "Of course we're going to have both." Seth shook his head. "As if that's even a question. Though first—" He bent down to retrieve the box he had placed on the floor when he was greeted by Jonathan. "—we need to have a taste of these."

"What's in there?" Jonathan had to admit, he was a bit curious. The box was bright orange with a black floral pattern printed in the middle of the lid.

"Samples of every kind of cake my favorite bakery makes." Seth's eyes were gleaming now. "This way we can console Leeland and have a first taste test for the wedding cake."

"Clever thinking, man." Jonathan raised a brow. "How many samples are there?"

"About thirty? They have a great variety."

"You do know Collin will never be able to choose one?"

Seth shrugged. "It's a multitiered cake. He doesn't have to choose one. He can choose up to five."

"Unless he can have all thirty, presenting him with so many options is almost cruel."

Now Seth looked a bit insecure. "Do you think? Perhaps I should take some of them out…."

When he started looking for a place where he could put the box down, Jonathan stopped him with an arm on his shoulder.

"It's okay, Seth. Just don't tell them it's for the wedding. The others will probably figure it out, but Collin is very—trusting. Just say you couldn't decide what to bring and everything will be fine. Then you can watch Collin and the others to see which cakes they like the most and, voila, you have the wedding cake all figured out without stressing Collin."

"You're a genius! Thank you, that's what I'm going to do. Emilio, you have to help me out. You keep an eye on Curtis and Peyton while I watch Dean, Collin, and Leeland. Would you do that?"

Jonathan watched as Emilio smiled shyly and nodded. Since he'd started dating Garrett, the boy had come a long way. Jonathan had to admit he found Emilio attractive. Not as hot as Leeland, of course, but enough to grasp Jonathan's attention. He led the two into the living room, where they were enthusiastically greeted and immediately drawn into the pancakes vs. cookies discussion.

Jonathan glanced at Leeland. His boy was still a bit pale, but the presence of his friends had obviously done wonders. Leeland could smile and laugh already, even if there was still a hint of despair in his eyes. Jonathan was positive it would be gone by evening. He left the boys to their discussion and sweets and went into his small office next to the master bedroom—the only room to escape Peyton's makeover of the apartment—to get some of his paperwork done. He didn't want to go down into the garage where his mechanics were working in case Leeland needed him here. Staying in the apartment also meant he could check in on the boys now and then and maybe help them with all the treats they had brought. It was a Dom's somber duty to be there for subs in need, and the boys certainly needed somebody to save them from sugar overload. Jonathan was determined to sacrifice his waistline to do just that.

Four hours, two films, two dozen pancakes, three batches of cookies, three ice-cream containers, and countless cake samples later, the bell rang again. Jonathan had just ended his third call with Richard and Martin, discussing security measures for Leeland. They had decided to have four bodyguards watching the apartment in shifts, and two assigned to follow Leeland wherever he went. Since he didn't plan on letting his boy out of his sight anytime soon, Jonathan felt this was a bit much, but Martin and Richard insisted. They had also, briefly, wondered if they should keep the bodyguards a secret from Leeland to not add to his worries. Knowing his boy, Jonathan had opted against it. Leeland wouldn't appreciate being left in the dark.

Jonathan reached the door and found Garrett on the other side when he opened it. His personal trainer and fellow Dom patted him heavily on the shoulder.

"I heard from Emilio. I'm sorry, man. This is really fucked-up."

Jonathan returned the gesture. "I know. Thanks. Come in."

"I'm here to get Emilio. I have a training session scheduled with him, and then it's dinner."

"Uhmm—to be honest, I'm not sure if he's going to be able to move a lot today… or have a meal. They've been eating for hours."

Garrett raised a brow. "Let me guess, it wasn't carrot sticks and low-fat yogurt dips."

"Your guess is correct. Leeland was very upset. He needed this." Jonathan wasn't sure whom he wanted to protect from Garrett's wrath—Emilio or himself. The man could be downright obnoxious when it came to food and what you should eat—or not.

Garrett sighed. "It's okay, Jonathan. I'm not going to punish anybody. I understand, I do. It's just—my boy has come so far. Seeing him fall back into bad habits saddens me."

They reached the kitchen, where Jonathan poured Garrett a glass of water. Before he could get himself a drink, he heard the bell again. Wondering who it was now, Jonathan went to the door. Greg stepped in, looking exhausted. He had bags under his eyes, and the laugh lines around the corners of his eyes and mouth seemed to be sharper than Jonathan remembered.

"Greg. Come in. Can I get you something to drink? How are things going?"

"A water would be nice. Is Leeland here?"

"Yes. His friends have come over to cheer him up."

Jonathan showed Greg into the kitchen, where Garrett rose from the stool at the breakfast bar. The two men shook hands.

"Garrett, this is Greg Smith, Leeland's trainer for the UFC. Greg, this is Garrett Kiernan, my personal trainer and boyfriend of one of Leeland's friends."

"Pleasure."

"Nice to meet you. I've only heard the best about you from Emilio. And sorry about your gym. Was it really arson?"

Consciously or not, Garrett was using his Dom voice to soothe Greg, who looked as if he was going to keel over any minute. Jonathan steered him to the second barstool, where Greg sank down.

"Yes. It was arson. And a hate crime. It's all gone. At the moment it looks as if they'll have to tear down the entire building because of structural problems. We've been talking to the police, the firefighters, the fire investigator, the people from Smash!, the insurance company, and, of course, dozens of reporters. At first there were only the local news channels, but as soon as social media got wind of it, the big ones came in as well. If one more person asks me if I think this is related to the upcoming fight, I'm going to knock them out."

Greg buried his face in his hands. "Misaki is frantic. He's trying not to show it, but I've known him long enough to see the signs. It's not only Leeland's training we need to reorganize, we need to find a place for Hinode as well. The insurance company isn't going to pay until the investigation is done, and for some reason Smash! isn't too forthcoming either. At the moment we're basically fucked."

Jonathan opened his mouth to comfort Greg when Garrett beat him to it.

"Emilio told me your gym is close to Little Havana. Is that correct?"

"Yes. We're the building at the corner. Or were." Greg sounded as tired as he looked.

"Well, I'm going to open a gym only two blocks from there in a week. Everything is more or less ready except for a few minor things.

You could do Leeland's training there, and if you explain to me who or what Hinode is, we can find a solution for that as well."

For the first time since he had come into the apartment, Greg looked hopeful.

"Hinode is Misaki's charity. He teaches street kids martial arts. At the moment there are thirty children in the program, aged twelve to seventeen, mainly boys. They can usually come over every day after school, but if we could have just two days, that would be great already. Just until we find a place."

"Nonsense." Garrett was talking in his take-charge voice now, one Jonathan usually hated hearing during training. It always meant he was going to be sore and sorry for himself. "My gym is big. We can easily have the children over every day. As for your other members, they are welcome as well. I'm sure we can work something out schedule-wise. That way you don't have to stress over finding a new place on top of everything else. You can concentrate on Leeland's training like you should, considering what he's going to be up against."

Greg stared at Garrett as if he couldn't believe the man, and Jonathan could relate. He knew that, under his gruff exterior, Garrett had a heart of gold; he just hadn't thought it was also as deep as a mine.

"Why are you doing this? I mean, thank you, but—why?" Greg seemed to fall over his own words.

Garrett shrugged as if what he had just offered was nothing.

"First of all, Leeland is a good friend to Emilio, and my boy needs friends like him. I'm grateful he has taken Emilio under his wing. Second, I like Leeland as well. He's a good man, one of us. He deserves all the help he can get, and he most certainly deserves beating that stupid asshole, Noah Adams. I'm not going to lie to you, this is also great publicity for me and my business. And I've been thinking about adding martial arts to my choice of courses in the gyms. The market is definitely there. Plus hosting a UFC fighter who is going to be in a championship fight? That is going to draw a lot of clientele in. We have to hash out the details, but with two experienced trainers like you and Misaki, I'm sure we can offer customers something unique. Perhaps you and Misaki might even decide to partner with me. Then you won't have to find a new gym."

Greg just stared with his mouth open. Jonathan had to hide a grin. Garrett might be acting as if his grand gesture was mostly business oriented, but Jonathan knew him better. Garrett Kiernan wanted to make his boy happy. Emilio admired Leeland, and by helping Leeland, Garrett made Emilio very happy. Martin had been right. The big, scary Dom was on his way to becoming a member of the sap club. Not that Jonathan would ever tell the man that to his face. He wasn't brave enough and enjoyed being able to walk after a training session.

Greg rose from his stool, grabbed Garrett's hand, and started shaking it like a madman.

"Thank you! Thank you! This is the first good thing happening today. I need to tell Misaki. You're taking a load off our shoulders. Thank you!"

Garrett smiled. "Why don't you call Misaki and ask him if we can meet at my gym? I can show you around, we'll talk, and see what needs to be done."

"Yes, yes. I'm calling him right now."

Greg hurried out of the kitchen to have some privacy. Garrett turned to Jonathan.

"Can Emilio stay a little longer? As soon as I'm done with Greg and Misaki, I'm going to pick him up."

Jonathan grinned. "Sure. I don't think he has a problem with that."

"Good. Don't tell them what Greg and I are up to. I don't want them to be disappointed if it doesn't work out."

Yes, sap club, welcome your new member. Jonathan tried to look serious and failed miserably, if Garrett's sour look was any indication.

"Misaki says he can get away from the police in twenty minutes." Greg sounded a bit breathless.

"Wonderful. Let's go. I'll give you the address. You pick Misaki up, and we'll meet at my gym."

Garrett and Greg hurried to the door. Jonathan saw them out and kept his fingers crossed that everything would work out.

CHAPTER 18

"COME ON, Leeland, one more round! Get your act together!"

Garrett's voice boomed through the training room, where Leeland was trying to keep Jonathan on the ground with the force of his thigh muscles alone. He imagined they looked funny, his big, burly Dom trying to wriggle out of Leeland's legs that were slung around his waist in a submission hold. Jonathan was strong and Leeland's thighs burned with the strain. He managed to hold on for another minute or so—to Leeland, it felt like an eternity—before he couldn't keep Jonathan down anymore. His Dom broke free and got on his feet. Leeland stayed on the ground, on his back, panting heavily.

"Not too bad, but you can do better!" Garrett was looming over him, his hand outstretched to help Leeland up.

"Why did Greg and Ojisan have to include you in my training? Why did you have to say yes?" Leeland knew he was whining and didn't care. He let Garrett pull him to his feet.

Garrett grinned. "I could say it's because I have a good heart and want to see you win, but we both know I'm a sadist down to my bones and enjoy making you squirm. I have to admit, though, you're tougher than your so-called Dom."

From the corner of his eye, Leeland saw Jonathan flip Garrett the bird, a gesture the other Dom responded to by maturely returning it. As gruff as Garrett pretended to be, Leeland knew he was invested in his training because he wanted to see him win. He was eternally grateful to Garrett for offering his gym after Misaki's place had burned down three weeks ago. Garrett, Misaki, and Greg had by now agreed to become partners. The news that Garrett had a UFC fighter and his trainers in his new gym made the member numbers skyrocket. Leeland was glad that Garrett's noble gesture benefited him. He wouldn't have known how to repay the kindness Garrett had shown—was still showing by helping with Leeland's training so Misaki could deal with all the tedious business regarding the fire. Investigations were still ongoing, though neither the arson investigator nor the police were forthcoming with how things were progressing, most probably because of the media attention the case was getting. The weirdest rumors were flying around, many of them linking the arson to the upcoming championship fight, though there was no proof Leeland knew of. Since the antigay pejoratives on the walls of the neighboring houses had been mixed with racial slurs, it wasn't clear who the arsonists had targeted: Leeland because he was gay, Greg because he was African American, or the gym in general because Misaki was helping the—mostly African American and Latino—neighborhood kids to escape their life on the streets. It wasn't even confirmed if this had been the doing of a single person or a group. Noah Adams had kept suspiciously quiet about the arson, only posting a statement that had clearly been formulated by his PR manager, saying he condemned this kind of behavior and felt for Leeland having lost his training base so shortly before the fight. If Leeland had cared more about what his opponent had to say, he might have been disheartened by the none-too-subtle dig at his inadequate preparation for the match, but as it was, he was simply glad that Noah didn't add fuel to the flames by spouting whatever nonsense came to his mind.

Despite the lack of official information, Leeland was glad how things had turned out. He even got to train with Jonathan at least twice a week. He suspected this was mainly because Garrett liked to see Jonathan suffer, but he wasn't complaining. Having three trainers breathing down his neck was decidedly exhausting, though combined with his determination to show Noah his place, his chances of winning were increasing. Leeland's parents had taught him to be modest but realistic about his talents, which helped him assess his chances without becoming overly confident or feeling discouraged.

"You're done for today. Get under the shower!"

Garrett's voice pried him from his musings. Leeland smiled when he saw Jonathan approaching him, hand outstretched, to take him to the showers.

"Not you, slacker!" Garrett sounded entirely too much like he was enjoying this. "You still have some weight lifting to do. We don't want to waste time while you're eating healthily. I know you'll be back to all that pig food you like so much as soon as Leeland's fight is over."

Leeland grinned and snuggled against Jonathan's—by now admittedly rock-hard—abs, stroking the muscles through the fabric of his shirt. He enjoyed how that made Jonathan shiver.

"Don't be mean, Garrett. I love my master the way he is."

"Thank you, boy." Jonathan kissed him on the temple.

Garrett snorted. "Do you want to do some extra rounds, Leeland?"

Leeland took a few hasty steps back from Jonathan. "No-o. Not really."

"Then I suggest you stop undermining my training, boy." Garrett raised a brow.

Leeland shot Jonathan an apologetic look before he backed toward the door. "I'm sorry, Jonathan. You heard my trainer. I have to go shower."

"Traitor," Jonathan mouthed, his own back turned to Garrett so he couldn't see him.

Leeland blushed, grinned, and ducked outside before Garrett could change his mind.

WHEN LEELAND came out of the shower twenty minutes later, he found Emilio changing next to his own locker.

"Hey, Emilio. What are you doing here?"

The shy young man turned to him with a smile. "Hey, Leeland. Master Garrett has asked me to come here for some extra training. He said since he's already here and it's on the way for me, we might as well squeeze in some extra time."

Leeland let his gaze roam over Emilio's bare chest. He was reaching for his T-shirt, and all the muscles moving smoothly under his bronze skin looked mouthwatering.

"The training becomes you. You have bulked up nicely."

Emilio blushed and ducked his head. "Thank you. Master says I still have a long way to go, though."

Like at a few occasions before, Leeland had the nagging feeling that something was wrong with how Emilio sounded. He wasn't unhappy, as far as Leeland could tell, but there was an undertone in his voice, one Leeland couldn't quite place.

"You know you can always tell him to back off a bit?"

Emilio blushed even harder.

"I know," he whispered. "It's stressful sometimes, but he really cares about me." Emilio was silent for a moment. "Nobody has cared for me in a very long time. I'm not going to jeopardize that. Not for anything."

Leeland simply pulled Emilio into a hug. The young man rarely talked about his time on the streets and never about what had happened between him and his parents. Having grown up with all the love and support a child could wish for, Leeland couldn't imagine what it was like not to have it and how that would affect one's social life and behavior.

"You have a lot of people who care for you, Emilio. You just have to let us. You're no longer alone, sweetie."

They both chuckled at the endearment Peyton usually used when he wanted something.

"I know, Leeland. And I'm grateful. It's just… landing somebody like Master Garrett is like a dream. When he first asked me to do a scene with him, I thought I'd swoon."

"How ladylike of you." Leeland tried to lighten the mood. It seemed to work, because Emilio pulled out of their embrace, smiling.

"Yeah." He shuddered. "Imagine what kind of impression that would have made."

"Only the best. There are dozens of Doms who like their subs on the fragile side."

"Not Master Garrett, though." Emilio sounded wistful while he looked down at his chiseled abs. If Leeland wasn't mistaken, he could see the beginnings of an eight-pack forming there. Garrett definitely knew what he was doing, even though he tended to get a bit extreme sometimes.

"No, not Master Garrett. Good thing you didn't swoon."

"Yeah, lucky me." Emilio glanced at his watch. "Damn. I only have fifteen minutes left to get warmed up. It was nice talking to you, Leeland. See you!"

He pulled on his shirt, grabbed a bottle of water, and was out the door before Leeland could say his goodbyes. Leeland wasn't offended. He, too, would never make Garrett wait. It just wasn't healthy. He wondered if he should talk to Garrett about Emilio's lack of self-confidence, his need to prove himself all the time. Then again, Garrett was a capable Dom, and he truly liked Emilio. If he hadn't figured out Emilio's problems by now, he didn't deserve to be with him. And perhaps all the relentless training was Garrett's way of trying to build Emilio's self-confidence? Leeland sighed. This wasn't a problem he could solve instantly. It would have to wait until after the fight was over and he could focus on finding out what exactly the issue was.

He started rummaging in his bag for the cocoa body butter Dean had given him a few days before. The moment he found it, his cell started to ring. Slightly annoyed, Leeland took it out from the side of the bag to look at the screen. When he read the name there, the frown on his face turned into a smile. He swiped the screen to accept the call.

"Hi, Carlos! How are you doing?"

"Hi, Leeland. I'm fine—more or less. I just wanted to know how your training is going? Is the sadist still bothering you?"

"I just had a session with him. I think he gets crueler every time we meet. Today he made me do submission holds for over an hour. I can't feel my thighs anymore."

"Poor you. I'd say I'll kiss it better, but your boyfriend would probably kill me if I tried."

They both laughed. Leeland enjoyed the playful banter between them immensely. Since the gym had burned down, Carlos had sent him at least one text every day in an attempt to cheer him up and had called every second day to lend his support. He obviously had no problem with Leeland being gay, which had restored Leeland's faith in humankind somewhat. Not all people were assholes. The assholes were just the ones who screamed loudest. Leeland was grateful for having found such a great new friend. And he loved talking to somebody who could relate to his situation.

"Yeah, better not. I like you the way you are—with all limbs attached." Leeland turned serious. "Is Mason still mad?"

Carlos's stepdad and trainer had gone ballistic when he heard Leeland would be fighting for the championship belt. Apparently he didn't like a fag, as he had put it, receiving that chance. Carlos had only reluctantly told Leeland about Mason's antics, not wanting to put further pressure on him, but Leeland had gathered from Carlos's strained tone that something was wrong and had insisted on knowing. He had come to the conclusion that Mason was a major idiot who didn't deserve working with an amazing fighter like Carlos.

"Yep. Not a day passes without him starting a rant about how he doesn't understand why Sean Shelby chose you to fight Noah Adams. He doesn't have a problem with Noah, though."

Leeland couldn't see Carlos but knew his friend was probably shuddering the same way he did. Noah was just nasty.

"Have you thought about my offer?" When it had become apparent how bad Mason was, Leeland had asked Carlos to come to Miami and meet his ojisan. He had to get away from that toxic man.

"Yes. And I think I'm going to take it. I'll wait till after your fight, then I'll come to Miami. I really can't stand listening to his homophobic slurs any longer."

"Great. Just give me the word."

"I will. And you focus on your training. You have an asshole to beat in two weeks."

"Thanks for the pep talk, coach. I appreciate it." Leeland said it in a serious tone. He was glad about Carlos's support. Even though he had the love and backing of his family and friends, the aid of a fellow athlete carried a special weight. More than Leeland would have thought. Of course there were quite a lot of UFC fighters who had congratulated Leeland on being out, but none of them had contacted him personally, not like Carlos. For that alone, Leeland would be forever grateful.

"You're welcome. I have some traveling to do the next three days, but I'll make sure to call you after that."

"Okay, Carlos. Have fun!"

"You too!"

They both ended the call, and Leeland finally started unscrewing the lid of his body butter. He was just about to scoop some of it up when a deep, sexy voice coming from behind stopped him.

"Wait, honey. Let me do that."

Leeland turned to see Jonathan standing in the door. He was dripping sweat.

"Oh my God, what did he do to you?"

Jonathan managed a weak grin. "Let's just say I'm going to do a happy dance when your fight is over and I don't have to see Garrett's ugly mug every day. Twice a week is more than enough. Or I could just change my personal trainer. That man loves torturing me way too much."

Leeland approached Jonathan to press a kiss to his lips. When Jonathan tried to embrace him, he jumped back with a squeal.

"Don't you dare! You're all sweaty and gross while I'm already showered."

"I thought you liked my manly scent?" Jonathan waggled his eyebrows. "And I still need to punish you for abandoning me before."

"I didn't abandon you. I just followed my common sense."

"And abandoned your master. I won't forget that, boy."

The teasing tone in Jonathan's voice, as well as the gleam in his eyes, told Leeland how much his lover enjoyed their banter. He let his eyes grow big and looked up to Jonathan in a pleading manner.

"I'm sorry, Master. Please, let me make it up to you. What do I have to do? I don't want you to be mad at me."

Before Leeland could duck out of reach again, Jonathan grabbed him around the waist and pulled him against his sweaty, stinking T-shirt.

"You could come and take a shower with me, for starters. That would please me greatly. After that, you could allow me to smear that body butter all over your skin. And then…."

Leeland's breathing grew heavy under Jonathan's suggestive look.

"Then we could do… other things, Master. Nice things. Nasty things."

"Oh yeah. Yeah, I like the idea."

They kissed, slowly, deeply, savoring how close they were, how good it felt to be in each other's arms.

"Let's shower."

The look of pure hunger on Jonathan's face sent shivers down Leeland's spine.

"Let's shower," he responded breathlessly.

CHAPTER 19

JONATHAN WATCHED as Leeland stepped on the scale for the official weighing. Camera shutters clicked like mad, lights flashed everywhere, and he couldn't suppress the twinge of jealousy when he saw all those strangers ogling his boyfriend's naked chest. The press conference before the weighing had been as terrible as Jonathan had expected, with Noah Adams openly insulting Leeland every time he opened his mouth, and the assembled reporters egging him on with the most stupid and obvious questions Jonathan had ever heard. Leeland stayed calm the entire time, smiled politely at the cameras, and answered the questions as seriously as if he were on a job interview. When Noah made another comment about Leeland's looks—so far he had complained about his smooth skin, his clothing, his full, long eyelashes, and the soft sheen on his lips that didn't come from lip gloss as Noah had insinuated, but from the intense make-out session Leeland and Jonathan had before the interview—this time saying how his long hair made him look like a little girl, Leeland turned to him with a broad smile. The room fell silent when the reporters realized Leeland was about to answer Noah directly.

"If you keep making so many comments about my looks, I have to assume you want to ask me out, but I'm sorry." Leeland put a finger to his lips and winked. "I'm already taken."

Noah opened and closed his mouth like a fish out of water, and a vein in his forehead started to throb. The whole room erupted in laughter, which only grew louder when one reporter asked Noah, "Well, do you want to ask him out? I wouldn't blame you. He looks gorgeous!"

Jonathan watched Noah clench his fists, ready to attack the reporter. Before he could jump the man, though, Noah's trainer leaned forward, put a hand on his shoulder, and whispered into his ear. For a moment Jonathan thought Noah would ignore whatever his trainer had told him and do something stupid enough to get him withdrawn from the fight and into custody, but then he bit his lip and relaxed slightly. After that Noah didn't make any more digs about Leeland's looks and acted almost professional.

Once the weighing was over, the opponents were free for the rest of the day to prepare for the fight the next evening. On their way to the car, Leeland, Jonathan, Misaki, and Greg met Noah and his entourage, who were waiting in front of the elevators. Noah's face contorted into a hateful mask, and Jonathan felt Leeland tensing. He slung his arm around Leeland's shoulders, knowing that would piss Noah off even more, but Jonathan was way past caring when it came to this idiot. All he wanted was to show his lover, his precious boy, that he wasn't alone. A light squeeze from Leeland showed how much he appreciated the gesture, and Jonathan felt his chest swell with pride.

"You!" Noah shouted like a madman. "You made me a laughingstock! How dare you?!"

Leeland shrugged. His tone was calm, a stark contrast to Noah's shouting. "You've been insulting and bad-mouthing me for months. Just because I have more class than to lower myself to your level doesn't mean I'm a pushover. Today you gave me an opening too good to pass up on. Thank you for that. And in case you're wondering, I really don't want to go out with you. I prefer real men over testosterone-driven wannabes."

For a moment all Noah could do was splutter, while Jonathan tried his best to hide his snicker. As much as he resented Noah, he didn't want to egg the man on further. Though on second thought, maybe he would blow a vessel, and then his boy wouldn't have to face him in the octagon. It was Misaki who ended the uncomfortable standoff between the two parties by grabbing Jonathan's elbow and leading him firmly away from the elevators.

"I think we're going to take the stairs. Good training."

Jonathan followed obediently, his arm still around Leeland's shoulders. Greg took up the rear. They were already a dozen feet away when Noah found his voice again.

"I'm going to destroy you, fag boy! Do you hear me? I'm going to pound your pretty face into the ground until not even your dirty boyfriend will recognize you anymore!"

They walked a little faster, Noah's hateful tirade ringing in their ears. When they reached the car, they quickly entered and waited for the driver to take the steering wheel after he had closed the doors. The black sedan rolled out of the underground parking lot and wove into the traffic of Las Vegas, bringing them back to the Bellagio, where Richard had rented an entire floor for their friends and family.

"That man is so full of shit." Greg was the first to break the silence.

"Do not listen to him, Leeland. All he has is his hatred." Misaki's words didn't quite match his furious expression.

"I don't." Jonathan felt Leeland shudder in his arms. "I just don't get it. Why does he have to be so nasty? I never did anything to him."

"Some people are just like that—only happy when they can pick on somebody. And even then, I don't think they're happy. Just no longer alone in their misery." Jonathan stroked Leeland's back. His boy leaned into the touch like a cat.

They talked some more about the upcoming fight and possible tactics Leeland could use, but that was basically just a repeat of what Misaki and Greg had already decided. The car stopped in front of the Bellagio, and they got out. Together they rode the elevator up to their floor, where Greg and Misaki turned to find Garrett's room while Jonathan took Leeland to the suite Smash! had booked for them. Now that their fighter was in the championship, they spared no expense. In case Leeland won, there would be a huge party in one of the ballrooms of the Bellagio. As soon as he knew where they would be staying, Richard had flexed his business muscles a bit to get them all together on the same floor. Quite a lot of members from Whisper would be there to support Leeland during the fight, and it made sense to keep the family together. Richard and several of the other Doms had also paid for the tickets and plane ride for the subs who couldn't afford such expenses. Jonathan felt a lump in his throat whenever he thought about the support Richard, Martin, and everybody at Whisper were showing Leeland.

He swiped his card to unlock the door to their suite and guided his very silent boy inside. They sat down on the luxurious sofa in cream and gold in front of the giant screen that dominated the living room. Leeland snuggled into Jonathan's side, his face buried in Jonathan's chest.

"Do you want to talk?" Jonathan spoke softly. He could feel how agitated Leeland was. His boy's nervous energy rolled off him in waves, making Jonathan's fingers itch to give him a spanking to calm him down. *Soon*, he reminded himself. Tomorrow evening the fight would be over, and he would have his lover back to himself. Jonathan hadn't lied when he told Martin he would support Leeland no matter what, but he was relieved nevertheless that this little field trip into the world of professional sports would be over soon.

Leeland pressed himself even closer. "Can we have a bath? And not talk? Just—can you hold me?"

Jonathan's heart went out to his lover. Leeland sounded vulnerable, almost lost. And it wasn't just the tension before the fight. It was the pressure Leeland felt from his uncle, from Smash!, from the LGBTQ community, who had started following Leeland after Noah Adams's rants had reached national level, and even, to some extent, from his friends and family, not to mention his own high expectations of himself. Nobody said it out loud, but they all wanted to see him win. For different reasons, obviously, but still. Jonathan didn't want to see Leeland win. Not anymore. All he wanted was for his boy to be happy again. To be able to relax and smile and be his old laid-back self. Leeland wasn't made for the world of MMA, where men hid behind their aggression, where being different was interpreted as weakness and showing emotion was forbidden. Jonathan was proud that he and Leeland—and their friends—had left this toxic interpretation of masculinity behind, and he was even prouder that Leeland didn't fall back on it to fit into the world of UFC. His boy was firm in his convictions, something that required more courage than a man like Noah Adams would ever possess.

"I'll hold you as long as you wish, boy."

Jonathan felt Leeland's gaze on him, hot and grateful. "Thank you, Master."

Together they went into the bathroom.

CHAPTER 20

LEELAND STOOD in front of the gate through which he would enter the T-Mobile Arena and watched the crowd go wild when Noah Adams entered the cage. The arena was packed, with at least two dozen rainbow flags being waved all over the arena. Leeland hadn't known that Leandra, the blogger who had been at his first interview and done some coverage in his favor, together with the people from some local LGBTQ groups, had organized a crowd of supporters for him. Now it wasn't only his family and friends out there—Jonathan had told him there were almost a hundred people from Whisper in the audience—but also a huge group of queer activists. It made Leeland happy knowing that he had so many people on his side.

Noah strutted into his corner, and Leeland heard his own name being announced. He stepped out into the light, almost staggering back from the massive wall of sound and different scents that hit him. Leeland let his gaze briefly wander over the crowd, making out Dean, Richard, Martin, his parents, and the people from Whisper, before he focused on the cage. When he entered, his eyes immediately found Jonathan, who was waiting in his corner, outside the cage. Leeland knew that without his Dom and lover, he would have cracked along the way. Jonathan had been his pillar of support, his safe haven in all this madness, and seeing him here through the bars of the cage, not cheering him on like mad, just giving him a slow, graceful nod full of trust and love, filled Leeland with pride and determination. Pride that this exceptional man had chosen him to be his partner. Determination to win this fight and then show Jonathan for the rest of their lives how much he loved him.

Leeland gave his man a quick smile before he turned to face his opponent. The referee had closed the cage and was now motioning them to come forward. When Leeland and Noah were only two feet apart, the referee blew his whistle and raised his hand.

The first round had begun.

Noah didn't waste time. He threw a direct punch toward Leeland's face, one he quickly ducked and answered with a sweep of his left leg. Noah stumbled but didn't fall. The crowd roared, pleased at getting so much action in the first seconds. Noah caught himself and rained a series of punches on Leeland's upper body, most of which he was able to block. A few landed, though, and they hurt like hell. Before Noah could start another volley of blows, Leeland stepped out of his range, turned, and attacked with a spinning kick that caught Noah in the chest and had him stumbling backward.

Leeland knew Noah had originally started with kickboxing before he turned to MMA. He hadn't done it long enough to become very good at it, which meant he had no stable base to rely on, unlike Leeland, who had several black belts in different martial arts as well as fighting experience.

Most UFC fighters came from a certain sport, be it boxing, wrestling, or a martial art, and many of them were well-trained in that particular sport, which could be an advantage. Having a set of movements so ingrained that one didn't have to think about it when using them could give a fighter the edge over an opponent like Noah, whose basics in all the different styles were solid, but who didn't have one specialty. This advantage could turn into a problem, though, if the fighter wasn't able to adapt to an opponent's fighting style or couldn't think outside the box of his original sport and react creatively to attacks.

At the moment Leeland had the upper hand because he simply allowed his body to go through a set of attacks he had used during his active time in high school. He managed to corner Noah, who didn't seem to know how to counteract the combination of kicks and blows Leeland rained on him.

Then the whistle announced the end of the first round. Leeland went into his corner, where his ojisan and Greg were waiting. Misaki was talking fast.

"You're doing good, but you've made him angry. He's going to be more forceful, so be careful. You know his punches are hard, and he's like a wounded bull now. Keep your guard up, wait for your chance, and then strike!"

Leeland nodded, his eyes glued to Jonathan on the other side of the cage bars, smiling at him. Nothing could have given him more strength than that look. For this moment alone, where their eyes met through the wire of the cage, Leeland was glad that his being gay was finally out. Not having the open support of Jonathan during the fights had been harder than his crazy athlete's diet. It made him realize how deep their relationship had become, that such a small gesture carried all the meaning he needed to keep going.

The whistle sounded again, and the second round began.

As his ojisan had predicted, Noah tried to get as many punches in as possible. One uppercut almost knocked Leeland out and had him staggering back. Noah saw his chance and went right after Leeland. He jumped high in the air, twisted slightly, and aimed his right arm at Leeland's back for an elbow strike. That kind of attack was particularly vicious and could open cuts or even bring an opponent down. Leeland ducked at the last possible moment, but he could still feel the rush of cold air when Noah's body brushed past his. While his opponent was still busy landing on his feet, Leeland got in one kick at his ribs and a second one at his thighs. The third one, aimed at Noah's face, was blocked, and they both danced back a few steps to regroup. Leeland could see Noah's chest heaving and knew the man was as exhausted as he. Noah was also furious, his face red not only from the strain, but also from anger. The unrestrained hatred Leeland could see in Noah's eyes made him shudder. It almost seemed as if the man was going mad.

Before they could go at each other again, the whistle blew.

Leeland was grateful for the one-minute break. Fighting was always strenuous, but this match against Noah was extracting everything from him. Again his ojisan started giving him advice.

"You need to end this, Leeland. Preferably in the next round. You can't take many more hits like the one from before. Be faster, be smarter, be harder! You can do it!"

Leeland didn't need his ojisan to explain to him that he wouldn't last another two rounds like this one, let alone three. He had to knock Noah out, no matter how. It was swinging for the fences or facing possible defeat.

When the whistle blew again and Leeland stood in front of Noah once more, his vision narrowed in on his opponent, and he felt the familiar focus that wiped everything beside the fight from his mind. He saw Noah lift his right fist to land a direct punch in his face, while the movement of his left shoulder indicated he was going for an uppercut. Leeland blocked the cut and brought his leg up, his knee hitting Noah under the rib cage, at the level of his kidneys. Noah gasped for air, his body twisting as the pain set in. Leeland had been at the receiving end of this maneuver before and knew he had to be fast now before his opponent could regain his senses.

He took two steps away from Noah to get some room. Then he went into a roundhouse kick, striking Noah square in the chest. The man swayed on his feet, clearly unable to defend himself at the moment. Leeland jumped, locked his feet around Noah's waist, twisted his body in the air, and sent them both to the mat, Noah in a submission hold between his legs.

The roar of the crowd was deafening. Leeland knew all he had to do now was to hang on until Noah tapped out. Noah didn't make it easy. He twisted like a worm on a hook, tried to punch Leeland, and landed a few good ones on his upper thighs that Leeland would feel for some time, but Leeland didn't let go. He just squeezed harder and harder from his superior position on top of Noah, forcing the air from Noah's lungs until he had no other choice than to tap the mat, which he did with an expression in his eyes that had Leeland shuddering. Never before had somebody looked at him with so much hatred and loathing in their eyes. All Leeland hoped for at that moment was that he would never ever see Noah Adams again.

The whistle sounded again, this time to mark the end of the fight.

Slowly Leeland got up. The referee came to him, grabbed his right wrist, and yanked it in the air.

Leeland had won.

He stood in the middle of the octagon, the cheers of the crowd washing over him, and tried to understand what had just happened. Rainbow confetti was raining down on him. Apparently many of the queer fans had come prepared for his victory, and rainbow-colored light sticks were lit everywhere in the arena. Two officials approached Leeland with the championship belt in their hands. They slung it around his waist before shaking his hand and congratulating him. He heard his ojisan and Greg laughing and cheering from somewhere beside him, but Leeland cared for only one voice in the cacophony erupting around him. And then Jonathan was there, right in front of him, with a broad smile on his lips and his arms opened wide. Leeland fell into his embrace, concentrating on the steady heartbeat in Jonathan's chest that soon drowned out the noise from the crowd. There, in the arms of the man he loved, his brain finally caught on.

He had won.

He had really won.

Leeland started crying. It was as if a chain that had been squeezing the air out of his lungs since he agreed to go pro had been taken away, and now all he could do was let all those pent-up emotions finally out. He didn't care that crying was considered unmanly and weak. Hell, he'd just proven his manliness by winning the championship belt. He was entitled to some tears. Jonathan seemed to sense the change in Leeland's body, because he tilted his head up with his right hand to look Leeland in the eyes. The love Leeland saw there through a veil of tears made his heart constrict. The world fell away when their lips met in a gentle, deep kiss that conveyed in this very moment what words could never hope to express.

Their private time was rudely interrupted when somebody grabbed him from behind and lifted him on Jonathan's shoulders. The world came back in all its overwhelming intensity. From his elevated position on Jonathan's shoulders, Leeland surveyed the crowd. He found his parents, who were cheering and laughing, hugging each other, and kissing openly. He saw Richard and Dean doing much the same, and Martin and Collin, who were both smiling so hard Leeland feared their faces would fall off. He had been worried when Collin announced he would come to his championship fight, remembering how badly the artist had reacted to his first match, but Martin had assured him the situation was under control, whatever that meant. At the time Leeland had been too preoccupied with the upcoming match to do more than accept Martin's word, though he decided to find out soon what exactly he had done to get Collin through watching the match. Emilio, Peyton, Seth, and Curtis were doing a silly victory dance, throwing rainbow-colored confetti and paper streamers in the air. All the members of Whisper had mixed with the LGTBQ part of the audience, celebrating like they had won the fight themselves—and in a way, they had. This was another step in opening professional sports to gay athletes. Leeland was under no illusion that things would instantly become better, but with each tiny—and not so tiny—step, the world turned into a better place for queer people.

Jonathan was slowly making his way toward the corridors, away from the crowd. When he reached the gate through which Leeland had come less than an hour ago, he helped him down from his shoulders, and together they went to the locker room where Leeland had changed. As soon as the door closed behind them, Leeland started kissing Jonathan frantically. Jonathan laughed through the kisses, a low, deep rumble in his chest that did funny things to Leeland's lower body. By all rights he should have been too exhausted to move, but the adrenaline coursing through his body made him feel like somebody had given him an IV filled with coffee.

"Do you want to have victory sex?" Jonathan's seductive tone did nothing to dampen Leeland's sudden lust.

"Can we?"

"It's your win, Leeland. Of course we can. Anything you want." Jonathan hesitated, pushed Leeland back a bit, and looked at him. "*Anything* you want," he stressed, and for a moment Leeland didn't understand what he meant. When it dawned on him, his eyes grew big, and he felt his heart overflowing with love. He went on tiptoe to kiss Jonathan on the nose.

"As much as your offer tempts me, what I really need is to feel you inside me."

Jonathan lifted a brow. "Are you sure? I don't know if I'm going to extend the offer beyond tonight."

The teasing tone told Leeland the offer was extended indefinitely.

"I'm sure. I want you now. The other thing—we can do that when the time is right. And I do want to do you, make no mistake. It's just, right now, I want to feel who I belong to."

Jonathan pulled him closer again. "You're mine, honey. Mine alone."

"Show me."

CHAPTER 21

A VERY long shower and some incredibly intense sex later, Jonathan watched Leeland get dressed for the interview. Luckily he had thought to lock the door so nobody could enter. The banging on the door had grown frantic during the last ten minutes, and Samantha Jones's voice was a shrill reminder that they had to go out and face the world soon. Sighing, Jonathan went over to Leeland, who was fidgeting with the buttons on his dark red shirt that made his skin glow. He smelled of lemon shampoo and cocoa body butter and, very faintly, of sex, which had Jonathan's possessive instincts flaring. His boy, his!

He helped Leeland with the buttons before he tilted his head back to examine the cut over Leeland's brow and the swelling on his left cheek. Noah Adams had gotten a few good punches in. When Jonathan thought about the bruises already forming on Leeland's perfect body, he felt his fingers twitching with the urge to strangle Noah. Jonathan had put arnica cream on all the places Leeland had been hit and had pressed a cold pack against his cheek to keep the swelling down. Despite his wounds, Leeland looked absolutely stunning, and if there hadn't been the interview and a party waiting, Jonathan would have brought him back to their hotel room immediately for a private celebration.

Instead he took his boy's hand, led him to the door of the locker room, and opened it. They were greeted by a slightly flustered Samantha Jones, who looked predatory in a bright red miniskirt, white blouse, and the highest heels Jonathan had ever seen. He was sure she needed a license for them, because they could easily stab somebody.

"What took you so long? Everybody is waiting for the winner! Come, shoo, shoo, we don't have time."

She pushed them through the endless corridors toward the press room, where indeed everybody was waiting. Jonathan saw cameras from CNN, Fox, of course, some local news stations, countless reporters for newspapers and magazines, as well as a slew of bloggers.

Samantha grabbed Leeland's wrist and dragged him to the table, where he was seated behind a forest of microphones. Jonathan waited to the side where he had a good view of his lover. The interview started with the usual. A female journalist asked: "Mr. Drake, how are you feeling after your victory?"

Leeland showed his most dazzling smile. "To be honest, I don't know. Exhausted, for sure; sore, definitely; happy, of course. I don't think I'll be able to fully grasp what has happened today until I've had a good night's sleep."

"Are you referring to the insults Noah Adams has so liberally spread on social media about you? How does it feel for you, as a gay man, to have won this championship?"

The question was from a bulky man in his late forties, if Jonathan had to guess, and from the way the man was smirking, Jonathan just knew he was expecting something juicy. Damn vultures!

Leeland furrowed his brow and chewed on his lip while he composed his answer. Jonathan could tell from the way his boy's shoulders had gone tense that he was contemplating if he should stay polite and evasive or if he should give an honest answer. Apparently honesty won.

"I don't see what one has to do with the other. Or, no, that's wrong. I do see what one has to do with the other, at least for the media and most people out there. But for me, these two things are separate. What Noah Adams said about me, and queer people in general, were terrible, hurtful insults against me as a person, and I resent him for it. Still, it wasn't the gay that won the fight today. It was me, Leeland Drake, a martial arts fighter who happens to be gay. The question is, what has my sexual orientation to do with my performance in the octagon? Nothing. Absolutely nothing. And I would wish those with power in professional sports would see it like that as well. Does being gay make me a better fighter? No. Does it make me a worse fighter? No, as you have all seen today. The things that define my fighting are my trainers, my body, my talent, and the people who support me. It has nothing to do with my sexual orientation. I didn't win as a gay man today. I won as an athlete who has put a lot of effort and hard work into getting where I am now. I'm aware that being gay and an athlete will be an issue for a long time to come. I just wish it wasn't, because it has no influence on the actual performance of the athlete except for the additional pressure everybody is putting on them." Leeland smiled again, this time with a hint of mischief. "And yes, I do feel a tiny bit smug about having beaten a man who seems to never think before he speaks."

The assembled journalists chuckled, clearly amused. They had a few more questions about the training and even the arson. Leeland managed to get Misaki's and Garrett's names in, which was great PR for them. Then the last question was announced, and it came from Leandra Donnell.

"Is it true that you're resigning now?"

Jonathan saw Leeland turn his head, and their gazes met. The smile on Leeland's face was one of pure joy and love.

"Yes, Leandra, that's true. I only acted as a stand-in for an injured athlete, and I can't wait to get back to actually eating something that isn't disgustingly healthy."

Again the journalists laughed. Leandra grinned. "I guess I know what you're going to do once you're out of this room."

Leeland didn't comment. He got up, and Jonathan hurried to his side. He could hear the shutters of countless cameras clicking, but it was the last time. It wouldn't take long for them to slip back into the anonymity of a normal life, and Jonathan couldn't wait.

They followed Samantha out of the arena to the car that would drive them back to the Bellagio, where Smash! had organized the party. When Samantha had finally realized that Leeland was friends with *the* Dean Connelly, best-selling author and husband to Richard Miller, one of the most influential businessmen in the US, as well as Collin Malloy, aka Rainbow Snake, she had gone out of her way to make them attend. Keeping Dean's and Collin's identities a secret from her hadn't been easy, but Richard and Martin had managed to do so until shortly before the championship match. How Samantha had connected the dots, Jonathan didn't know, and it didn't matter anymore. Leeland's time in the spotlight was almost over. Richard had originally planned on organizing his own party for Leeland, but when Samantha agreed to invite all the men from Whisper, he hadn't hesitated to leave it all to her.

And she had outdone herself. The party was tasteful, with a minimum of Smash! logos on the walls, waiters who carried champagne flutes through the crowd, and a delicious buffet with finger foods from all over the world. Of course, everybody wanted to congratulate Leeland and talk to him. Jonathan made sure to stay close to his boy, because he could see how the exhaustion was catching up with Leeland now that the adrenaline from the fight was finally starting to subside. It was still nice, though. Being among their family and friends, listening to the good-natured banter and heartfelt well-wishes, helped Jonathan to see all the good that had come with Leeland's time in the UFC, and it put the bad—the lack of time they had for each other, Noah Adams's homophobic rants, the fire in Misaki's gym—into perspective. Being with a professional athlete was not what Jonathan wanted to do for the rest of his life, but it had been an interesting experience.

They didn't last long. After two hours of hugs, handshakes, smiling, and nodding, Jonathan sensed that Leeland was close to falling over. He lifted his beautiful lover up and carried him bridal style, to a background of catcalls and whistles, to the elevator that would bring them to their suite.

It was time for bed.

CHAPTER 22

A week later

"THAT WAS perfect." Peyton stretched like a cat before he let himself fall down on the lounge next to Leeland. "You were right about the pedicure. I feel like I'm flying."

Leeland just grinned. At the moment Dean was getting a massage, Curtis was in the sauna with Emilio, Collin, and Seth, and he was waiting to be picked up for his own pedicure. Dean's idea to spend the day at the spa before having their movie night had been a stroke of genius. Leeland could get used to it. His fingers ghosted over his cheek. The swelling had gone down, and except for a light soreness here and there, Leeland felt as good as new.

"What film do you think Seth has chosen?" Leeland glanced over at Peyton, who was busy admiring his perfectly lacquered toenails. The mint green went surprisingly well with Peyton's lightly tanned skin.

"I have no idea. He's making a big secret out of it, which is kind of suspicious. I fear the worst."

Leeland snorted. "You always fear the worst."

"If Vin Diesel isn't in it, how can it be a good movie?"

"What about Viggo Mortensen? You like him well enough."

Peyton threw his hands in the air. "Fine. *Lord of the Rings* does have its moments."

Leeland grinned. Teasing Peyton was fun. "And I do remember you laughed quite a lot when we watched *The Stepford Wives*."

"As much as I hate to admit it, Nicole Kidman was actually good in that one. And I adore Bette Middler." Peyton threw Leeland a look. "And don't think I didn't see you wrinkling your nose when Emilio put on *Hocus Pocus*."

"That film is fine. It's just, ever since she played Carrie Bradshaw, I can't watch Sarah Jessica Parker in any other film. Always makes me think she's dressed like a slob. And you have to admit, those witch clothes aren't exactly flattering."

"You don't seem to have that problem with Sean Murray." Peyton folded his arms over his chest.

"Because he's a cat most of the time. No weird associations there."

"You associate Sean Murray with a black cat and think that's normal?"

"Shut up, Peyton."

Peyton stuck out his tongue. "Only because I've seen what you can do when you let loose."

"What are you two bickering about?"

Dean's voice had that faraway quality he got when he was either blissed out from a scene or had just had a full-body massage. Leeland knew this because Richard had once complained that Dean reacted to a scene the same way he did to a treatment. Leeland found that highly amusing, though he would never dare tell Richard to his face.

"We were just wondering what kind of film Seth has chosen for tonight." Peyton was back to looking at his toenails as if they were the most fascinating thing he'd ever seen.

"We'll find out soon enough." Dean shrugged. The massage had obviously relaxed him completely. "It can't be worse than some of the movies you've put us through." He looked pointedly at Peyton, who rolled his eyes in his best drama-queen mode.

"Why are you all criticizing my taste in films?"

"Because the films you like are, unlike the houses you design, trash."

Curtis's smooth British accent stood out, as always. Leeland loved the way Curtis talked. He could listen to the man for hours. That he also had a beautiful, full voice only added to the charm.

"Boys, why don't you sit down and enjoy the peace and quiet?" Seth interrupted, putting emphasis on the words "peace" and "quiet." "You'll find out soon enough what kind of movie I've chosen, and I promise you, you'll like it."

"Peyton says that *every* time we come over to his place, and it has yet to happen. You have to give us a bit more." Leeland grinned broadly. Teasing Seth was almost as much fun as teasing Peyton.

Seth just flipped him off. "Emilio, do you want to go for a swim? I feel the need to get away from these bickering bitches."

"Who-ho, bickering bitches! What an alliteration!" Dean was laughing so hard, his body shook with the effort.

Emilio looked between Seth, Peyton, and Leeland, shrugged, and grabbed a fresh towel from his bag.

"Okay, let's go. I do have permission to eat as much as I want tonight, but a little extra training surely won't hurt."

Leeland saw Seth's expression freeze. "Uhm, Emilio, I meant swimming as in 'paddling around while talking,' not as in actually, you know, *swimming*." Seth sounded a bit frantic.

Emilio grinned. "Too late. Besides, a bit of training never comes amiss."

He started sauntering toward the outside pool, giving them all a full view of his taut little ass. Groaning, Seth hurried after him. Dean shoved Leeland until he could sit down at the side of his lounge. "Damn. All that training looks good on him." He made a face. "Though I think lately he sounds a bit too much like Garrett."

Leeland grinned halfheartedly. He still wasn't sure what to make of Emilio's relationship with Garrett. On the outside everything seemed perfect. Emilio was thriving under the attention of his strict master and seemed to be perfectly happy, but Leeland couldn't shake the nagging feeling that something was not as it should be. He just couldn't put his finger on it, and it drove him crazy.

"I liked the sauna. It was hot but good. Do you think we could build one ourselves? There's this spot in our backyard that could do with a little something, and I could try and build a real sweat hut with logs and everything, and Curtis, did you know wood is such a great material to work with, I have so many ideas what to do with it, only Martin says I can't have a chain saw, but I really need one, and can you explain to him how important that is?"

Collin looked at Curtis with puppy eyes. Curtis sighed and patted the younger man on the shoulder.

"I'll see what I can do for you, but really, Collin, chain saws are dangerous. I think you should find somebody to teach you first. Maybe then Martin wouldn't be as averse to the idea."

Collin beamed. "That's a great idea! I'm going to ask Mike and Jeff. They know everything about tools!" He turned, no doubt to get his cell and call the two men, but Curtis stopped him.

"Don't you think that can wait until tomorrow? Our hara massage is in ten minutes, and then we only have one more hour to relax before we have to face whatever movie Seth has chosen for us."

Collin seemed torn, which had Leeland biting his lips to keep himself from laughing. He always enjoyed Collin's enthusiasm for learning and expanding his knowledge.

"Fine. Massage first. But I'll call them tomorrow as soon as I wake up!"

Curtis and Collin waved at Leeland, Dean, and Peyton before they went to get their massage. Five minutes later Leeland was picked up for his pedicure, and two hours after that, they entered Seth's apartment for the first time.

It mirrored Seth perfectly. His home was close to the Keys, and the front window in his living room looked out onto the water. On the ground level, everything was open except for a small bathroom, which made the place look bigger than it was. A stair led up to the second floor, where the bedroom and a huge bathroom with a walk-in shower and a Jacuzzi tub were located. The last room served as an office/storage room, which had Peyton visibly cringing. He hated nothing more than wasting perfect living space. Amused, Leeland watched as the interior designer tried to keep his mouth shut. Seth's tastes ran toward masculine elegance, with a hint of something more playful here and there. The massive black leather couch would have probably smothered the room if it weren't for the colorfully quilted cushions on it, each of them unique. The huge flat-screen TV with the PlayStation and the impressive surround-sound system screamed man cave but was countered by the sewing machine in the corner. All in all, Leeland found Seth's apartment quite cozy and could easily imagine them spending more time there.

They had decided against going to a restaurant and had gotten takeout instead. With the exception of Curtis, none of the others had eaten Afghan food before, so Seth insisted they try it. If the mouthwatering smells coming from the containers were anything to go by, Leeland didn't think they would regret their decision.

"What's for dessert?" Collin looked expectantly at Seth. Dessert was important and not to be trifled with.

Leeland saw Seth winking at Collin.

"Remember all those little cake samples I brought when we comforted Leeland?"

Collin nodded eagerly, and Leeland perked up too. Those cakes had been delicious.

"Well, they had a lot of spare samples because a customer canceled at the last minute, and I took them all. I think it's enough for all of us to eat our body weight in cake."

"Oh, how nice!" Dean beamed at Seth. "No matter what kind of movie we're going to watch, you're forgiven."

"Have a little faith, won't you?" Seth grinned. "I'm going to get the cutlery. You make yourselves comfortable."

Once they were all seated and eating happily, for the food was truly good, Seth glanced around.

"Are you ready?"

"What have you planned?" Curtis sounded a bit nervous. He was still afraid Seth would turn out to be another action film fan, like Peyton. Seth put his fork down.

"First of all, I want to thank you for including me in your group. You're all great guys, and I enjoy spending time with you."

"Flattery won't save you when your choice of film is bad," Peyton interrupted Seth, barely hiding his laugh. "And since you're talking sweet like that, I assume you know some of us won't like it!" Now he was laughing outright.

Seth growled and shot him an angry look. Leeland just leaned back, enjoyed his food, and listened to the bantering.

"I just wanted to set the right mood," defended Seth. "As I said, I like you all, and during the course of the past few months, I think I've gotten a pretty good insight of what you like and dislike. The film I chose is actually a series. It's considered a classic by many—" Seth nodded toward Curtis "—has a suitable amount of action—" He looked at Peyton. "—a good sense of humor—" This was addressed to Dean and Collin. "—a heroine who has emancipated herself from the confines of society, and an absolutely crazy story line." Seth gestured to

Leeland and Emilio. Leeland wasn't sure what to think. This sounded way too good to be true—a film they all equally liked.

"What's the catch? Is it in Finnish with English subtitles?" It seemed as if Dean shared Leeland's suspicion.

Seth shook his head. "Oh no, it's a true American series from the late nineties and early two thousands."

"Stop drawing this out! Just tell us!"

As usual, Peyton was the first to run out of patience. Seth held his hands up in a dramatic gesture.

"Ladies and…, sorry, gentlemen and gentlemen, I give you— *Buffy the Vampire Slayer*!"

The reaction to that announcement was a mixed chorus of "Oh no!", "Wow, cool!", "I haven't seen that in ages!", and "What's a slayer?" The last came from Curtis, who obviously had no clue what *Buffy* was. Leeland took pity on him.

"*Buffy* is a series about a teenage girl who has special powers and kills vampires and demons. Joss Whedon created her because he took pity on all the beautiful, blonde girls who were always the first to die in horror movies. The series is indeed considered a classic by many and said to have given the figure of the vampire a new twist."

Curtis furrowed his brow. "Shouldn't we have read *Dracula*, then, before watching this?"

"No, no, no, no need for that!" Peyton practically screamed. If there was one thing Peyton abhorred, it was reading the original before watching a movie to lend a "deeper meaning to the discussion," as Curtis liked to put it. It was one of the reasons why Dean and Leeland had seriously discussed watching *Game of Thrones*—just to see Peyton squirm. Not only Doms could be cruel.

"And you think I'm going to enjoy this?" Curtis regarded Seth with a puzzled look.

"Did I mention there's a slew of good-looking, scorching-hot guys on the show as well? And two of them are British!"

"Being British doesn't automatically make for a good performance." Now Curtis sounded indignant.

"Spike only starts in season two—though he *is* hot. Can we start with season two?" Peyton begged. Leeland decided to end this before they spent the whole evening discussing a film Curtis hadn't even seen yet.

"How about we start with season one, just to get the background right for those of us who haven't seen it or have forgotten about it?"

Seth rose from the couch, patted him on the shoulder on his way to the TV, and started fumbling with the DVD.

They watched the first two episodes, then took a break to clear away the takeout cartons and get the cake samples before watching another three episodes. Curtis did warm up to the series quickly, though to Leeland's surprise, his favorite character was Cordelia, not Giles. Curtis was a man of many mysteries.

It was almost one in the morning when they finally said their good-byes. Collin was driving with Dean and Peyton, and Emilio was with Curtis. Leeland got behind the steering wheel of his Volvo and sent a quick text to Jonathan that he was on his way. This late at night, Jonathan wanted to know when Leeland got behind the wheel so he didn't have to worry—or rather, so he knew when to start worrying. Leeland loved him for it. He started the engine to get home to his man.

CHAPTER 23

"SO WHAT'S my big surprise?"

Jonathan glanced at his lover, who was squirming in the passenger's seat. After their training with Garrett—now back to only twice a week, and Jonathan definitely didn't complain—he had suggested they shower together. His boy was sharp enough, though, to realize something was going on when Jonathan started cleaning him thoroughly. Leeland had nagged him until he admitted there was a surprise waiting at home. Now his boy was asking every few minutes on their way back to the apartment. Jonathan found it adorable.

When they arrived, he parked, opened the car door for Leeland, and led him up the stairs to their home. Leeland was practically vibrating.

"I thought for sure the surprise would be at Whisper."

Jonathan grinned. "Nice try, boy." He opened the door and put on his Dom face. "Strip. The scene starts now."

"Yes, Master." Leeland lowered his gaze, but not before Jonathan had seen the hunger in his eyes. His boy was eager. Jonathan felt his cock responding to this mixture of obedience and need.

It didn't take Leeland long to get rid of all his clothes. Jonathan nodded his approval.

"Hands behind your head, eyes down. We're on high protocol. Your safeword?"

"Dust bunny for red, dandelion for slow down, pasture for go."

"Very good, boy. Follow me."

He started walking without looking back, knowing his boy would do exactly as he was told. On his way down the hall past their bedroom to the guest room, Jonathan got rid of his own shirt, which had Leeland moaning softly. If Leeland was surprised that they didn't go to their bedroom, he didn't comment. Like the perfect sub he was, he just accepted it. Jonathan couldn't suppress a smile when he opened the door to the guest room and saw everything had turned out the way he had planned. More than a dozen candles burned on various flat surfaces in the room. In the middle of the room stood a massage table, and on it was Thomas, naked, on his back, his hands tied to the legs of the table at each side. Next to Thomas stood Don, the owner of Leathers, the shop where most of the members of Whisper bought their gear, in black leather trousers and nothing else. On a small table to the right side of Thomas's head lay the equipment they would need for tonight.

"Hello, Don, Thomas. It looks perfect in here."

Don smiled and took Jonathan's outstretched hand. "Thank you. You prepared it perfectly. All we had to do was light the candles. Hello, Leeland."

Leeland acknowledged Don's presence with a slight bow of his head, nothing more. Jonathan knew if his boy wanted to, he could follow protocol down to a T.

"Shall we begin?" Don's gaze wandered down Leeland's beautiful body and stopped at the leaking hard-on. Jonathan grinned, filled with a strange sense of ownership pride. This was his boy, his lover, and it pleased him that a Dom as seasoned as Don appreciated Leeland's perfect body.

"Yes, let's start." He turned to Leeland. "On your knees, boy, legs spread. Hands stay where they are. You're allowed to watch, but no sounds, understood? And no coming either." The last Jonathan said with a hint of wickedness to his tone. He had meant it when he said the scene started the moment they got through the door.

When Leeland was on his knees in perfect position, Don gestured for Jonathan to come over. "Ready?"

Jonathan nodded. He was grateful Don and Thomas had agreed to this private demonstration. Of all the things Leeland had to sacrifice for his stint in the UFC, going to Whisper and attending demonstrations had been among the hardest, and Jonathan remembered all too well the night when he almost went to the sounding demonstration without his boy. He had promised him they would go together, and tonight he was making good on his promise.

"Yes, I'm ready."

Don nodded. "Good. First, go to the bathroom and wash your hands with the antibacterial soap there."

Jonathan did as he was told and came back into the room doctor style, not touching the knob on the door. Don held a box with surgical gloves out to him. Jonathan put them on and stepped next to Don. Don started to speak.

"The most important thing in sounding is keeping everything as clean as possible." He grabbed a bottle of alcoholic sanitizer from the small table and sprayed it generously on Thomas's groin. Like Leeland, Thomas was hard as nails, and he winced when the cold liquid hit his cock. Don looked at his boy.

"Your safewords, boy?"

Thomas whimpered. "Moneypenny for stop, Moonraker for slow down, Connery for go."

"Good boy." Don grabbed Thomas's cock and sprayed the tip, which had Thomas groaning. Don put the spray back on the table. Then he took a tube of sterile lube and opened it. He grabbed Thomas's dick again and manipulated the cockhead until the slit looked like an O before pouring the lube into it.

"Anything that goes into your boy's urethra needs to be sterile. Otherwise you risk an infection or warts or even long-term damage. If you don't have sterile lube or you aren't sure if the sounds have been properly sterilized, you don't do a sounding scene. That's the beginning and end of it." Don selected a thin metal rod with a sphere at the end. "You start small," he explained while he carefully positioned the tip of the metal at Thomas's slit, "and don't use excessive pressure. You don't want to tear anything or even create a dead end in your boy's urethra. If he has to have a catheter for medicinal reasons and there is a dead end, the catheter can't reach the bladder. As you can see, the tip is round, and everything is smooth. As long as you're careful, nothing bad can happen."

Don started slowly, carefully, pressing the metal rod down. Thomas moaned and whimpered, doing his best to keep still. Jonathan glanced at Leeland, who was watching the scene with huge eyes. His boy's face and chest were flushed, his breathing heavy, and there was a small puddle of precum on the floor between his spread knees.

"When the rod is in a good position, you let the weight of the sphere do the rest of the work," Don explained. He was now simply keeping the sound upright while it slid deeper into Thomas's body, seemingly of its own accord. "When the rod stops, you do not push it deeper. Slide it out, add more lube, and then go in again. Always slowly, always in controlled movements." He demonstrated what he meant by pulling the sound out and squirting more lube into Thomas's slit before letting go of the sound again. Thomas was panting. With a smile, Don pulled the sound out completely. The desperate whimper from Thomas's lips had Jonathan's cock hardening to the point of pain. Don turned to him.

"Now you try it." He handed him a slightly thicker sound.

Jonathan inhaled deeply before he took Don's place. He was grateful for the older Dom's presence and that he allowed him to try this on Thomas first. Otherwise Jonathan wasn't sure if he would have had the courage to do it. Under no circumstances did he want to hurt Leeland. He took Thomas's cock, manipulated the tip as Don had, and positioned the sound.

"Remember, slow movements, no pressure." Don's voice sounded calm from somewhere behind Jonathan's left shoulder.

Jonathan let the sound sink inside Thomas's slit, allowing the sphere at the end to do the work. When the sound was completely in, Jonathan looked at Leeland. To his utter joy, he saw Leeland's gaze was fixed on his hands, following every movement Jonathan made. If Jonathan had to guess, he'd say his boy was imagining himself on the massage table. Don stepped next to him to inspect his work.

"Good job. Do you want to try and give Thomas one more, or do you want to work on your own boy?"

One look at Leeland made the decision easy. "My boy."

"Okay. Go wash your hands again and put on fresh gloves. I'll untie Thomas."

Jonathan hurried to the bathroom. While he washed his hands, he heard Don talking to Thomas through the half-open bathroom door.

"You're such a good boy. So brave. You deserve a reward, my sweet one."

Jonathan smiled at his reflection in the mirror. He hoped he and Leeland would still be so in love after such a long time as Don and Thomas clearly were.

When he came back to the room, Leeland was already on the massage table. Don looked at Jonathan.

"Do you want to tie him up?"

Jonathan shook his head. "No. This isn't about obedience. It's about us."

The radiant smile he got from his boy told him he'd made the right decision. From the corner of his eye he saw Thomas, who was now kneeling in Leeland's place with the sound still in his cock, trying to keep a straight face and failing miserably. Don just grumbled something about lovesick fools who needed to toughen up, which caused Thomas to roll his eyes, something Don didn't see, or otherwise Jonathan was sure he would have gotten some punishment.

"Now, remember what I told you." Don opened a second metal box with a fresh set of sounds. Jonathan sprayed a generous amount of sanitizer on Leeland's groin, took a fresh tube of sterilized lube, wrapped his hand around Leeland's slim, elegant cock, and stroked it a few times before grabbing the tip. When he squirted the lube on Leeland's slit, his boy's moans grew in intensity and his hips lifted slightly from the table. Don placed a steadying hand on Leeland's stomach.

"Easy, boy. Try to stay down."

Leeland whimpered. "Yes, Master Don."

Jonathan smiled. He could feel Leeland's excitement, and it fueled his own. Slowly, carefully, he inserted the tip of the sound. Leeland made a noise between a pained sob and a desperate whimper. Jonathan stopped, waiting for his boy to adjust to the new sensation before he let the sound slip deeper. It took a while and a bit more lube, but finally the sphere at the end of the sound reached the slit. Jonathan felt dizzy with pride. He'd done it! He felt Don's hand on his shoulder.

"Very good, Jonathan. Do you want me to stay for one more sound, or shall Thomas and I leave?"

Jonathan hesitated. He wanted to be alone with his boy, but he didn't feel confident enough to be on his own yet. Luckily, Don seemed to sense his dilemma.

"Why don't I go to the living room with my boy and fuck his brains out? If anything happens, you just have to call and I'll be here in a heartbeat. Or once I've pulled out of Thomas's delectable ass."

Jonathan sighed happily, ignoring the dirty talk from Don and the needy whimper it elicited from Thomas. "Thank you, Don. That's a great idea."

From the corner of his eye, Jonathan saw Leeland fighting to keep his mouth shut. Knowing what worried his boy, he added: "Could you both use condoms? Otherwise Leeland won't be able to relax, I'm afraid."

After a moment of silence, Don simply lifted an eyebrow and nodded. Jonathan breathed a sigh of relief.

"I'm going to take my boy on the floor. Less messy, and he likes that, don't you, Thomas?"

A desperate moan was the answer to that.

"We'll leave you two alone."

Jonathan watched Don and Thomas leave the room. As soon as the door clicked shut, he turned back to Leeland, who was chewing his lip.

"What?"

"I wonder if you should have mentioned where the detergent is."

Jonathan couldn't help himself. He started to laugh. This was his boy, with all his strange little quirks, and Jonathan was so grateful to have him.

"If they leave a mess, I promise I'm going to clean it up. Can we get with the program now?"

Leeland let go of his lip. A hungry gleam entered his eyes. "Oh yes!"

"So glad you're still with me." Jonathan stroked the pretty cock with the sphere sticking out obscenely from the tip. "You're so beautiful. Now, shall we change to a bigger sound, or should we just have fun with this one?"

Jonathan had meant it as a rhetorical question; still, Leeland answered perfectly. "Whatever you wish, Master."

Jonathan bent down and kissed Leeland deeply. "I think this one's good. Let's have some fun."

With that, he started trailing kisses down Leeland's torso toward his twitching dick. When he reached it, he nibbled along the entire length, which drew an avalanche of moans from Leeland. Encouraged by this enthusiastic reaction, Jonathan held Leeland's cock with one hand while he licked up and down as if it were a popsicle. His boy's taste was slightly muddied by the gloves' rubbery scent, so he took a moment to get rid of them. Since he didn't plan on using another sound, he didn't need them anymore.

After a few moments of intense licking, Leeland's cock tasted of nothing but Leeland. Satisfied, Jonathan grabbed his boy's ankles, pulled until his ass hung over the edge of the massage table, and then knelt down, draping Leeland's legs over his shoulders. Seeing his beautiful lover so completely exposed had Jonathan almost coming in his pants. With an impatient gesture, he opened the fly of his jeans and freed his own cock. Then he went back to playing with his boy. He licked Leeland's balls, alternately sucking them into his mouth until Leeland's desperate pleas for more turned into incoherent gibberish. Jonathan then let his tongue wander farther down until he reached his boy's delicious hole. It was already twitching madly in anticipation and eagerly swallowed Jonathan's tongue when he pressed it against the rim. Since he was received so readily, Jonathan didn't waste time being careful. He plundered Leeland's hole with his tongue and lips, his boy's cries growing louder with every sweep he did inside his hot channel.

Finally, Jonathan was no longer able to control himself. He rose, found the tube with the sterile lube, slathered it on his own desperately leaking erection, positioned himself, and entered Leeland with one powerful thrust. They both cried out, craving the intimacy of this connection with a hunger they had suppressed for the past months.

"So good, boy, so good. Finally, us again."

"Jonathan, harder. Fuck me like you mean it!"

It didn't take more for Jonathan to lose the last shreds of control. He grabbed Leeland's hips so hard he was sure there would be bruises and pumped into him with his full strength. Leeland urged him on with groans and high-pitched squeals that told Jonathan exactly how good his boy felt. All too soon he felt the tingling in his balls and Leeland panted, "Close, Jonathan, so close. Can't... the sound!"

Jonathan managed to grab the sphere. He faltered in his relentless rhythm for a moment while he pulled it out before he started pumping again, this time in short, brutal stabs that had Leeland arching his back. At the same time Leeland shouted out his release. Jonathan felt his own cock twitching deep inside his boy's hot channel, filling it with his cum.

It took them both several minutes until they came down from their high, but when they did, they grinned at each other like madmen, full of love and satisfaction. Jonathan leaned forward to kiss Leeland, their tongues engaging in a slow, sensual dance that had his cock perking up again. When Jonathan broke the kiss and looked into Leeland's eyes, he saw something there, a tenderness that engulfed him with its warmth. Jonathan felt Leeland's fingertips brush over his cheek before his perfect, wonderful boy opened his lips to speak.

"Will you marry me, Jonathan?"

Jonathan was so stunned, he lost command over his larynx for a moment. Leeland's eyes widened.

"Did I just say that out loud?"

The horrified tone broke the spell over Jonathan's voice box. He grinned. "Yes, honey, you did. I guess my little slip when asking you to move in with me during aftercare is forgotten now?"

For a moment Leeland seemed confused. Then he lifted a brow, apparently remembering that particular scene. There was a challenging tone to his reply. "Depends on your answer."

Jonathan turned serious. "You know the answer, honey. It can never be anything else but yes. I love you so much, I'd be honored to be your husband."

"Good. You're forgiven." Despite the snarky words, Leeland was just as serious as Jonathan.

They smiled at each other, and Jonathan felt so full of love, he thought his heart would overflow.

"Seems like we really suck when it comes to timing. Could be difficult with the wedding."

Leeland arched a brow. "I know a wedding planner now. I'm sure Seth will see to it that everything works out." He sucked on his lower lip as if contemplating something. "We'd probably have to decide whether we want to wait until Collin and Martin have done the deed or if we want to do it right away."

"Do they have a date yet?"

"Not as far as I know. Though I think Seth already has most of the ceremony planned out. He's a sneaky bastard, using every chance

to have Collin make a decision without him being aware of doing it."
Leeland looked pointedly at Jonathan. "Don't think I didn't realize
what the cake samples were for."

Jonathan chuckled and kissed his boy on the tip of his nose.
"When did you find out?"

"I have to admit, it took me some time. I was a bit preoccupied
that day. It hit me the morning after, under the shower."

"My clever boy. I'm so proud of you!"

"Don't patronize me. Back to the question at hand—are we
going to wait?"

Jonathan thought about it for a few moments. "I like the idea of
being engaged to you. We can go and find a beautiful ring, have an
engagement party, bask in our promise. Then, if Collin and Martin
don't manage to tie the knot until the end of next year, we can have
our ceremony. How does that sound?"

"Like a brilliant idea from a smart man."

The cheeky smile his boy threw at him was enough to get
Jonathan interested in a second round. Since his cock was still inside
Leeland, Jonathan decided to indulge. He leaned down to kiss his
boy's sensual lips, while he stimulated his cock and balls at the same
time. Leeland whimpered.

"So good, Jonathan, so good. Give me more."

And just like that, Jonathan was rock-hard again, ready to give
his sweet lover, his fiancé, another good pounding.

EPILOGUE

"I WONDER how long it'll take Carlos to get his luggage."

"Huh?" Leeland looked up from his left ring finger, where his gorgeous ring was blinking in the sunlight that filtered through the huge windows of MIA. They were waiting for Carlos. After Leeland's victory, Carlos had come to Miami to meet Misaki and Greg and talk about joining their gym as a professional fighter. They had quickly come to an understanding, with Garrett backing up their decision. As of next month, Carlos would be an official member of Misaki's UFC team, together with two more athletes who were hoping for a successful career under his ojisan's tutelage. For the time being, Carlos would live with Greg and work as a boxing instructor for Garrett's and Misaki's gym. Once the new season started, he would go back to being a full-time fighter.

"I said, I wonder how long it will take Carlos to get his luggage." Leeland saw the laughter in Jonathan's eyes and shrugged. He was way too happy to feel insulted.

"Probably some time. He has at least four suitcases, or so he's told me." He went back to staring at his ring. They had gotten it four weeks ago in a little antique shop downtown. It was from the 1920s, a simple band made of blackened silver with three rubies worked into it. Leeland had seen the ring and immediately fallen in love. When it turned out it fitted him perfectly, Jonathan had bought it without hesitation, though he did complain that Leeland's attention was mostly on the ring now.

"You're in love with the ring, aren't you?" Jonathan's voice was soft, full of love.

"I'm in love with you. And the ring represents our love. So yes, I'm in love with the ring. Did you know this is the first time I've gotten a ring from a man?"

"Yes, honey. You've told me so a dozen times, don't you remember?"

"I might have forgotten about it." Leeland lifted his head so Jonathan could give him a kiss. Just when their lips met, Leeland saw Carlos coming from the baggage claim out of the corner of his eye. He stepped away from Jonathan and started waving frantically. The moment Carlos saw him, his face lit up. He started running, abandoning the cart with four huge suitcases on it in favor of embracing Leeland.

When they separated, Leeland saw that Jonathan had taken the cart, probably to avoid a bomb warning. Unattended luggage could ruin a perfect afternoon.

"Carlos, may I introduce you to my fiancé, Jonathan White."

Carlos shook hands with Jonathan. "Pleased to meet you, Jonathan."

"The pleasure is all mine." Jonathan seemed genuinely pleased. When Carlos had come to Miami two months ago to talk to Misaki, Jonathan had been on a business trip, and they had missed each other.

"Thank you for picking me up, Leeland."

Leeland patted Carlos on the back. "No problem. Greg is very sorry, but the gym is so busy, it's hard for him or Misaki to get off, and Jonathan and I were free. Anyway," Leeland smiled, "I wanted to see you as soon as possible. Look!" He shoved his left hand in Carlos's face. "How do you like it?"

Carlos seemed a bit confused until he spotted the ring. Behind Leeland, Jonathan chuckled.

"You better say something nice about that ring, or he won't stop pestering you until we've dropped you at Greg's place."

Leeland pouted. He knew it wasn't very mature, but when it came to his ring, he tended to be a bit extreme.

"It's beautiful, Leeland. Brings out the color of your eyes."

Leeland searched Carlos's face and found nothing but sincerity there. He felt his face light up. "Thank you, Carlos. I like it very much. Do you want to grab something to eat before we leave, or are you good to go?"

Carlos made a face. "I'm good to go. I'm hoping to get something decent once I'm at Greg's. He said something about eating out tonight."

Leeland felt his eyes grow big. "Greg is taking you out? For a real meal? When did hell freeze over?"

Carlos grinned. "Yesterday, apparently. And it's not as if I'm competing at the moment. I can slack off a bit."

Leeland simply shrugged. "I'm so glad this is behind me. There were moments I could have murdered somebody for a bar of chocolate."

"But you didn't. Thanks to Collin, I think." Jonathan leaned in from the side to kiss Leeland on the cheek.

Carlos shot him an inquisitive look. "What does that mean?"

Leeland patted Carlos on the back. "Nothing. Just that I have friends who dearly love me. Enough to help me cheat here and there when things got too rough."

"You think they would want to become my friends as well?"

Leeland smiled broadly. "I'm sure they will. Here we are."

They had reached the Volvo. Together they loaded the four heavy suitcases into the trunk before Jonathan drove them to Greg's apartment. During the trip, Carlos wanted to know everything Leeland knew about the arson at his ojisan's gym. Shortly after the championship fight, the arson investigator had made a breakthrough and found the culprits, some heavily misguided fans of Noah Adams who had taken his homophobic slurs too seriously and decided to act on them. As they found out quickly, burning down a building simply because their idol didn't like the occupants didn't save them from going to jail. They probably would have never been found if they hadn't bragged about their terrible act on Noah's Facebook. Apparently the idiots never died out. Then again, they might have felt encouraged by the daily hate speeches Noah posted on all his social media accountants. Losing against Leeland had obviously been a blow to Noah's ego. He had fired his trainer and was now at a MMA gym in Texas that was supported by an antigay televangelist and his church. And Noah could use some divine intervention, since the police were breathing down his neck because of the arson in Misaki's gym and his hate rhetoric. His future at the UFC was unsure as well. Through the grapevine, Leeland had heard that Dana White was seriously considering not offering Noah a new contract for the next season if he didn't apologize for his behavior. Leeland thought it might be best if Noah lost his official platform as a UFC fighter, but it wasn't likely. There would be some half-assed superficial apology written by Noah's new PR manager, and then he would keep on spewing his hatred at every official function he could get into. The thought had Leeland slightly depressed but not for long. He had a friend to settle in.

When they reached the apartment, Leeland opened the door with the key he had gotten from Greg before handing it to Carlos.

"Let me give you the tour. I can help with the unpacking, if you want."

Carlos smiled. "Thank you, Leeland. Give me the tour, but I think I want to do the unpacking alone. I need some time to digest my new situation."

Carlos didn't have to say more. Leeland knew how nasty the professional and personal breakup between Carlos and his stepfather had been. Mason hadn't reacted well to his stepson leaving him to train with Misaki. There had been many harsh, hurtful words, and Carlos had lost the only family he'd had left. Leeland still hoped Carlos and Mason would be able to mend some fences once Mason had calmed down, but he wasn't holding his breath. Mason wasn't a pleasant man to begin with, and losing Carlos seemed to have set his worst side free, if what Carlos had told Leeland was anything to go by. He was just glad Carlos had managed to leave Mason when he still had the chance.

"It's okay, Carlos. I understand."

Leeland showed his friend around while Jonathan waited patiently in Greg's living room. Once Carlos knew where everything was, they said their goodbyes and drove back home.

"Is he going to be okay?" Jonathan sounded worried. Leeland looked at his lover. This was the reason he loved the man so much. Jonathan might seem intimidating and harsh, but he had a good heart and cared deeply for others.

"Yes, I think so. He's a fighter, not just in the octagon. He'll pull through. And he has me now."

Leeland saw a smile blossom on Jonathan's lips. "That's right." He made the last turn before their apartment came in sight.

"Do you miss it? Competing, I mean?"

Leeland didn't even have to think about his answer. "No. Definitely not. I did this for my oji, not because I had a burning desire to get back in the ring. As you may have noticed, all that alpha male posturing isn't my thing. The only thing I'm going to miss a tiny bit is that shiny championship belt currently hanging in our closet." He paused for dramatic effect. "Then again, probably not. It's not really my style."

Jonathan laughed. "No, it doesn't suit you. You look far better in leathers of my choosing."

Leeland's cock gave an interested twitch at those words. "Which leathers would you choose for me to wear? I'm asking purely out of curiosity, of course."

Jonathan drove the car into the garage before he turned to Leeland. The look he gave him was so scorching hot, Leeland thought he would melt in the seat.

"Why don't we find out?"

"Oh yes, let's."

They left the car and went up to their apartment, hand in hand, and Leeland knew, if anybody asked him about the most perfect moment in his life, the answer would be every moment he spent with Jonathan. He looked at his wonderful lover and soon-to-be husband.

"I love you, Jonathan."

Jonathan gave him a kiss on the nose.

"And I love you, Leeland."

XENIA MELZER was born and raised in a small village in the south of Bavaria. As one of nature's true chocoholics, she's always in search of the perfect chocolate experience. So far, she's had about a dozen truly remarkable ones. Despite having been in close proximity to the mountains all her life, she has never understood why so many people think snow sports are fun. There are neither chocolate nor horses involved and it's cold by definition, so where's the sense? She does not like beer either and has never been to the Oktoberfest—no quality chocolate there.

Even though her mind is preoccupied with various stories most of the time, Xenia has managed to get through school and university with surprisingly good grades. Right after school she met her one true love who showed her that reality is capable of producing some truly amazing love stories itself.

While she was having her two children, she started writing down the most persistent stories in her head as a way of relieving mommy-related stress symptoms. As it turned out, the stress relief has now become a source of the same, albeit a positive one.

When she's not writing, she translates other authors' manuscripts to German, enjoys riding and running, spending time with her kids, and dancing with her husband.

Website: www.xeniamelzer.com
Email: info@xeniamelzer.com

A DOM AND HIS WRITER

XENIA MELZER

CLUB WHISPER

A Club Whisper Novel

Life is perfect for Richard and Dean. Richard is a wealthy and successful businessman who also owns a BDSM club, and Dean is a best-selling author and sub to Richard. They're young, happy, and in love. The future is bright….

Until tragedy strikes and an accident claims Dean's beloved sister. Dean finds himself the guardian of a three-month-old infant, and soon he's trading in his leather fetish gear for diapers and drool bibs. But little Emily is all that remains of his family, so how can he abandon her?

It's not what Richard signed up for. As much as he tries to be supportive, he never wanted kids and misses having his partner to himself. Suddenly the life he imagined for them is gone, and he's not sure their relationship can survive the upheaval. But fate isn't through with Dean, and when misfortune strikes again, will he be able to turn to the man he loves? A final crisis will determine if they can pull together as a family or must face facts and part ways.

www.dreamspinnerpress.com

A DOM
AND
HIS
ARTIST

XENIA
MELZER

CLUB WHISPER

A Club Whisper Novel

Sometimes the perfect man can be found in the most unexpected place….

Martin Carmichael owns a security firm and is part owner of Club Whisper. He's a Dom in search of the right guy, and when his car breaks down on a lonely stretch of road, he thinks he might have found him.

Artist Collin Malloy is talented, easygoing, but somewhat insecure. Still, he has a big heart and is quick to offer help when he sees Martin in need. To thank him, Martin invites Collin to dinner, where the attraction between them becomes harder to resist.

But what will become of their budding relationship when Martin reveals that he likes his men bound, submissive, and in pain? Is it something Collin can accept… and possibly enjoy exploring? Even if he can, Collin has a secret of his own—a secret he doesn't even realize he's keeping.

www.dreamspinnerpress.com

www.ingramcontent.com/pod-product-compliance
Lightning Source LLC
Chambersburg PA
CBHW060056260626
47160CB00005B/1684